AN IMPOSSIBLE OATH?

"I'm really ashamed that Phil's horse can do something Belle can't—especially when it's a dressage movement," Stevie said. "But I solemnly promise you, the next time Phil sees Belle, she'll be doing flying changes." She raised her hand like a Girl Scout taking an oath.

Lisa stifled an urge to giggle. "But Stevie, that doesn't give you or Belle much time," she reminded her friend. "Aren't you planning a picnic ride for Phil's birthday?"

Stevie nodded. "Two and a half weeks," she said. "Should be plenty of time. Deborah learned to ride as a wedding present for Max. I'll teach Belle flying changes as a birthday present for Phil."

"I bet he'd rather have a new halter," Lisa said.

"Flying changes," Stevie repeated grimly. "Two weeks."

THE SADDLE CLUB

FLYING HORSE

BONNIE BRYANT

A BANTAM SKYLARK BOOK
NEW YORK · TORONTO · LONDON · SYDNEY · AUCKLAND

I want to thank Eve Jordan for inspiring this story
one afternoon in Maratea. And thanks, too,
to Nancy Moore Hoeflich for her helpful memories
of Chincoteague and Assateague.

RL 5, 009–012

FLYING HORSE

A Bantam Skylark Book / August 1995

Skylark Books is a registered trademark of Bantam Books,
a division of Bantam Doubleday Dell Publishing Group, Inc.
Registered in U.S. Patent and Trademark Office and elsewhere.

"The Saddle Club" is a registered trademark of Bonnie Bryant Hiller.
The Saddle Club design / logo, which consists of
a riding crop and a riding hat, is a
trademark of Bantam Books.

ISBN 0-553-48264-5

Published simultaneously in the United States and Canada

Bantam Books are published by Bantam Books, a division of Bantam Doubleday Dell
Publishing Group, Inc. Its trademark, consisting of the words "Bantam Books" and
the portrayal of a rooster, is Registered in U.S. Patent and Trademark Office and in
other countries. Marca Registrada. Bantam Books, 1540 Broadway, New York, New
York 10036.

PRINTED IN THE UNITED STATES OF AMERICA
OPM   0 9 8 7 6 5 4 3 2 1

I would like to express my special thanks to Kimberly Brubaker Bradley for her help in the writing of this book.

"ISN'T THIS DAY just perfect?" asked Stevie Lake. She threw her arms open wide and sniffed happily at the fresh early-morning air.

"I don't know about perfect," said one of Stevie's two best friends, Lisa Atwood, with a slight smile. "I woke up late and didn't have time for breakfast, I couldn't find my boot hooks, and Prancer's thrown a shoe so I'm going to have to ride Delilah instead."

"Oh." Stevie's grin faded in sympathy. "I'm sorry about Prancer, Lisa. Are you sure—"

"I'm sure," Lisa said. "The shoe's come all the way off, and she's lost it in the pasture somewhere. It

1

wasn't even loose yesterday. I don't want to hurt her by trying to ride her without it."

"Not a Thoroughbred," Stevie agreed. The two girls belonged to a Pony Club called Horse Wise, in which they learned all sorts of things about horse care and training. They knew that while some horses had strong hooves and could be ridden without shoes, Thoroughbreds tended to have weak hooves. Prancer was a Thoroughbred and an ex-racehorse. "Don't be disappointed," Stevie comforted her friend. "You'll have a nice ride on Delilah. The trails will be gorgeous, no matter what."

"I know," said Lisa. "I wouldn't miss this trip for anything." Horse Wise had been invited by a neighboring Pony Club, Cross County, to go on a trail ride through Cross County's hunt territory. Lisa, Stevie, and their other best friend, Carole, had ridden at Cross County before, but they hadn't explored all the hunt trails. They loved to ride somewhere new.

"I wouldn't miss it for anything, either," said Stevie, the rapturous smile returning to her face.

Lisa laughed. "That's because the woods will be so beautiful, I'm sure," she teased. "Or maybe because you'll be riding your beautiful horse, Belle? It wouldn't have anything to do with Phil Marsten, would it, Stevie?" Phil was Stevie's boyfriend and a member of

Cross County. Lisa knew how rarely the two got to see each other.

"Like I said," Stevie responded, "this is a perfect day!"

"Up, up, up!" Across the yard of Pine Hollow Stables, Red O'Malley, the head stable hand, was helping Veronica diAngelo load her mare into the horse van. Garnet stepped daintily aboard on Red's command, and Stevie saw Red and Veronica exchange grins—a rare event, since Veronica was a spoiled brat and usually tried to boss Red around. Of course, Veronica had been treating Red a little more nicely ever since his girlfriend, Denise McCaskill, had come to help out at Pine Hollow. Veronica greatly admired Denise. Still—

"Would you look at that!" Stevie said.

Lisa nodded. "Veronica's helping load Garnet. She's even smiling. I can't believe it!"

"It must be something in the air," declared Stevie. "This really is an amazing day!"

"Except that without my boot hooks I can't pull my boots on," Lisa reminded her. She pointed to the tennis shoes she was wearing with her breeches.

"Switch to cowboy boots, they're easier," Stevie advised. "But I bet Carole is wearing her dress boots today. She'll have some boot hooks." She steered Lisa into the stable. They found Carole Hanson in the main aisle, wrapping shipping bandages around the legs of her horse, Starlight.

"Boot hooks?" Carole repeated vaguely. She straightened, patting Starlight's neck absentmindedly, and half closed her eyes. "In my cubby, in the tack room, second shelf, toward the back behind the saddle soap on the left-hand side." Lisa and Stevie grinned. Carole could be incredibly flaky, but she was always organized around horses.

"And Lisa didn't get to eat breakfast," Stevie continued.

"There are doughnuts. Maybe in the tack room? Somewhere." Carole looked around distractedly.

"Here?" Stevie plucked a pile of shipping bandages off a hay bale to reveal a bag of doughnuts.

"There." Carole smiled and went back to wrapping Starlight's legs.

"See?" Stevie said to Lisa. "Carole helps you out, and I help Carole help you out."

Lisa laughed. That was the best part of their threesome—not the way their personalities fit, which they certainly did, but the way they were always ready to help each other. They had even formed a club called The Saddle Club. Members had to be horse crazy and had to help each other out whenever help was needed. Both of those rules were easy to follow for Lisa, Carole, and Stevie.

4

"Starlight looks beautiful," Lisa said when she returned from the tack room with her boots on and her arms full of Delilah's tack. Lisa didn't have her own horse. She wanted one, of course, but she still wasn't sure she knew enough to give one the care and training it would need. Lisa hadn't been riding as long as Carole and Stevie, and although she was a good rider, she was also a good enough student to realize how much she didn't know.

In the stall next to Delilah's, Jessica Adler was saddling Penny, one of Pine Hollow's lesson ponies. "I can hardly wait," Jessica told Lisa as she walked Penny out of the stall. "I've never taken Penny on a real trail ride before." Lisa smiled. Now that she had her boots on and had eaten something, she was starting to feel enthusiastic about riding Delilah. The mare was sweet and would be nearly as much fun to ride as Prancer. The clear sky promised them a warm day, and a balmy summer breeze wafted through the stable, mixing with the smells of horses, leather, and hay. Lisa buckled the throatlatch of Delilah's halter and paused to stroke the mare's golden neck before leading her out of her stall. Stevie was right. This was going to be fun.

Outside, confusion reigned. Nearly a dozen Pony Clubbers were going to Cross County, but only four horses had been loaded onto the van. Red was standing by the van's ramp, trying to organize the horses that were ready to load. It was a short trip so the horses were traveling fully tacked. Denise was inspecting the horses' tack before they were put on board. Some of the younger riders hadn't put their saddles on properly or fastened the saddle girths correctly. A few of the ponies had gotten tired of waiting and were beginning to act up. Their riders shrieked and scolded.

Polly Giacomin ran through the crowd saying, "Oh gosh, how could I forget—" Her purple windbreaker flapped loudly in the breeze. The noise spooked Penny, who was just about to step onto the van. Penny backed up, fast, yanking the reins out of Jessica's hands. The pony wheeled and trotted briskly back to the barn.

"Jessica, what do you think you're doing?" A loud voice boomed across the yard. Instantly the riders went still. Max Regnery, owner of Pine Hollow Stables and leader of the Pony Club, strode forward angrily. Everyone looked shocked. Max could be a stern instructor, but he never yelled like that, especially not at one of the younger kids.

"She was trying to put Penny on the van," May Grover, one of Jessica's friends, said stoutly. "Polly ran past and made Penny nervous."

"I'm sorry, Max," Jessica said. "I didn't mean to let go of the reins, but I couldn't help it." Denise came back from the barn leading the pony. She handed Penny to Jessica with an understanding smile.

"Well," Max said grumpily. "You shouldn't have let it happen. All of you are making too much noise. It's no wonder the horses are upset. Let's have a little peace and quiet around here for once, okay?"

"Geez," said Stevie, leading Belle up beside Starlight and Delilah. "What's gotten into Max?"

"I don't know," said Carole. "I've never heard him talk to one of the little kids like that. He knows Penny doesn't like to go into the van."

"He must be missing Deborah," Lisa guessed. Deborah was Max's new wife. As soon as they'd gotten home from their honeymoon in London, Deborah, a newspaper reporter, had returned to Europe to cover a political summit. She'd been gone for a week already.

"It's awful to be separated from the person you really care about," Stevie said with a sigh. "I know what that's like."

Carole and Lisa rolled their eyes. "Well, I don't," Lisa said, laughing at Stevie's dramatics. "But I do know we'll never get to Cross County until the horses are on the van."

Carole nodded. "This is a job for The Saddle Club!"

In a minute they had everything organized. Stevie held Belle and Starlight while Lisa loaded Delilah, and Carole helped Jessica with Penny. Then Stevie and

Carole loaded their horses, and Lisa helped Denise finish inspecting the younger kids' ponies. Soon Horse Wise was ready to roll. "Here comes the most perfect part of the perfect day," Stevie said as they left Pine Hollow.

STEVIE WAS CERTAINLY right about one thing, Carole thought. The trails through the Cross County hunt territory were beautiful. Wide paths cut through pine woods and opened onto meadows and sparkling, sunlit streams. Starlight moved forward at a loose, relaxed walk. He seemed to appreciate the beauty as much as she did.

"This is wonderful," said Lisa. Carole nodded. They rode side by side, just behind Stevie and Phil. Delilah seemed as contented as Starlight.

Stevie thought she'd never been so happy. Just as she'd said, it was a perfect day. The woods were gorgeous, the weather was gorgeous, and Phil—well, Phil was gorgeous, too.

"I have to hand it to you, Stevie Lake," Phil said. "I've learned so much since I've gotten to know you."

Stevie turned to smile at him, blushing.

"I mean it," Phil persisted. "Without you, I would never have studied dressage. But since you were so involved in it, I got more interested, and it's been a big help in my riding."

8

Stevie grinned. Although she loved it when Phil said romantic things to her, riding was a more usual topic of conversation between them. Dressage was a highly technical sort of riding, without jumping, that Stevie loved and was very good at. "If I remember right, you got interested in it at about the same time our Pony Clubs had a dressage competition," she said. "You wanted to beat me." She was glad she could tease Phil about it. Sometimes the natural competitiveness between them got out of hand and made their relationship difficult.

Phil laughed. "But if I remember correctly, *you* beat *me*," he said. "But honestly, Stevie, I'm serious. I didn't realize that dressage training could be such a big help with my cross-country riding. Lately Teddy and I have spent a lot of time practicing flying changes, and it's really helped him to stay balanced when we're galloping on the trails here. Sometimes the paths twist awfully tightly, and now he can do a flying change whenever he needs to, and keep his legs underneath him."

Stevie knew that whenever a horse cantered or galloped, it led off with one of its front legs. The lead leg, or lead, was supposed to be the leg on the inside of the direction the horse was turning. For example, the right leg should lead when the horse turned to the right, so that the horse would be better balanced through the turn. The rider told the horse which lead to take when they started cantering, but if the horse needed to switch leads there were two ways to do it. In a simple lead change, the rider asked the horse to slow to a trot and then pick up a canter on the other lead. In a flying lead change, or flying change, the horse switched leads midcanter.

"I'll show you," Phil offered. "Watch." He pushed Teddy into a canter, then lengthened the horse's stride to a balanced hand-gallop. Once Phil established a good forward pace, he and Teddy proceeded to do several flying changes on the flat, smooth trail. Teddy's bulky frame became elegant—suddenly he looked as if he were dancing.

"Wow!" said Carole, just behind Stevie.

Stevie nodded. "*Wow* is right."

"I saw," said Lisa. "Those were flying changes, right?"

"Every couple of strides, and on a straightaway, too," said Carole. "That's really impressive. I didn't know Phil could ride like that."

"Neither did I," said Stevie in a small voice.

Phil trotted Teddy back to them, his face flushed with pride. "What did you think?" he asked them.

"That was really something," Stevie told him honestly. "I bet you're pretty proud of Teddy, too. I didn't know he could do that."

Phil patted his horse's neck. "Neither did I, until I asked him to try," he said. "But you're right, I do feel pretty proud of him."

THE REST OF the ride, in Lisa and Carole's minds, was every bit as glorious as the start, but they couldn't help noticing that Stevie seemed less and less euphoric. In fact, by the end, she didn't even seem to be having fun, and her good-bye to Phil was uncharacteristically subdued. On the car ride home they confronted their friend.

"What's up?" Lisa asked. "This morning you were higher than a helium balloon, and now you look like someone's popped you. You couldn't have had a fight with Phil, we were right behind you the whole time. What's wrong?"

"I don't know." Stevie scraped some mud off her boot heel with her fingernail.

"You know you can always tell us," Carole reminded her. "If something's bothering you, we want to help."

Stevie looked up, and her friends were surprised at her agonized expression. "It's Belle," she whispered.

"Something's wrong with Belle?" Carole was instantly concerned. "But Stevie, she looked fine—"

"No, she's fine. It's just"—Stevie lowered her voice

so that the other passengers couldn't hear—"she doesn't know how to do a flying change."

Lisa would have laughed if she hadn't known how serious Stevie was. "Stevie, that's not exactly a problem. It's not like she kicks people, or rears, or has colic or something."

"I'm just so embarrassed," Stevie countered. "I'm really ashamed that Phil's horse can do something Belle can't—especially when it's a dressage movement! Lisa, you know I'm better than he is at dressage."

Lisa wisely didn't respond. Stevie always fought to be a better rider than Phil. It had caused her problems before.

"Stevie," Carole said sensibly. "You act like it's a major fault, when really it's just a lack of training. You can certainly teach Belle to do a flying change."

Stevie nodded her head. "Oh, I will," she assured them. "In fact, I solemnly promise you, the next time Phil sees Belle, she'll be doing flying changes." She raised her hand like a Girl Scout taking an oath.

Lisa stifled an urge to giggle. "But Stevie, that doesn't give you or Belle much time," she reminded her friend. "Aren't you planning a picnic ride for Phil's birthday?"

Stevie nodded. "Two and a half weeks," she said. "Should be plenty of time. Deborah learned to ride as a wedding present for Max. I'll teach Belle flying changes as a birthday present for Phil."

"I bet he'd rather have a new halter," Lisa said.

"Flying changes," Stevie repeated grimly. "Two weeks."

LISA RAN UP the driveway of Pine Hollow. She could see Carole and Stevie already mounted, along with the rest of the students in her Tuesday-afternoon lesson. Lisa tried to run faster, but her side hurt. "I'm sorry, Max, I'll be right there," she gasped from the side of the ring.

Max looked fierce. "You of all people I don't expect to be late," he told her. "Lisa, you know how I feel about coming to lessons on time."

"But I had a dentist appointment, and the dentist was late," Lisa explained, "and my mom couldn't pick me up, so I had to walk from downtown Willow Creek, and there weren't any buses—"

14

"All these excuses are only making you later," Max replied. "If I were you, I'd be tacking up Prancer instead of standing here talking." He turned on his heel and clapped his hands at the rest of the class. "Let's trot!" he commanded.

Lisa had to blink back tears. She felt stunned. Max had never spoken to her like that before. She knew he hated having his students arrive late for lessons, but he always listened to her. She couldn't remember his ever being angry at her for something she couldn't help. Lisa fled to the stable, unaware of the concerned looks her friends sent after her.

Running through the door, Lisa nearly collided with Denise McCaskill, who was coming out of the office with her arms full of clean stable sheets. "Whoa!" said Denise. "Lisa, what's wrong?"

"Oh, everything," said Lisa. "I'm sorry, Denise. I shouldn't be running in the stable, I know. But I'm so late for my lesson, and Max is angry—"

Denise put the sheets down on a bench. "I'll help you," she offered. "Who're you riding?"

"Prancer," she said, gulping.

"You get her tack, and I'll put her on the cross-ties."

When Lisa got back, Denise had already brushed Prancer and was picking out her hooves. "Thank you so much, Denise," Lisa said. "I've had the worst day."

"I can see that," Denise said sympathetically. "Here, hand me the saddle pad. What's wrong?"

"Oh, dentist, and my mom was too busy to drive me, and I couldn't find a bus—I've had a whole bunch of days like this lately, and I almost never do." Lisa helped Denise settle Prancer's saddle across her back. "Max is just furious, and I don't know why."

"He's been like that lately," Denise replied. "I don't know if it's because Deborah is gone, or what. Today he bawled Red out, and Red still isn't sure why. I wouldn't take it personally, if I were you."

"It's just that this is summer," said Lisa. "It's supposed to be the best part of the year, and it's starting out really crummy." She put the reins around Prancer's neck and began to bridle her.

"I always feel a little displaced this time of year, too," said Denise. "College is out but I haven't really gotten into the swing of vacation. It seems like all the fun summer stuff happens later, in July or August. This time of year I always want to do something different, but I never know what it is."

"I'd like something different," said Lisa as she gave Prancer a final check, "I'd like not to be late for this lesson. Thanks again for your help."

"Good luck!" Denise replied. "And Lisa—chin up!"

The class was still trotting in its two-point positions, the way Max liked to warm up students and

16

horses, when Lisa entered the ring. He didn't say a word to her, or even look in her direction. Lisa checked her girth, mounted, and quickly started trotting. She still felt embarrassed about Max's yelling at her.

"Lisa, look out!" Stevie shrieked. Lisa sat back just as Belle cut the corner at a flying gallop and nearly ran into Prancer's side. Prancer laid her ears back, but, thanks to Stevie's warning, Lisa kept her under control.

"Stevie, what was that about?" demanded Max.

"She spooked—the wind blew a piece of paper into the ring—" Stevie sputtered. Stevie got Belle back into a trot, but it was clear that the mare was fighting her. Lisa sighed. This on top of everything. Lisa knew from riding Prancer that some days high-strung horses could be flighty. Belle was usually calm, but not today.

Stevie was so upset she didn't know what to do. She'd been worrying about Belle ever since Saturday's ride, and in this, their next lesson, Belle was being *horrible*. There was no better word to describe it. The mare seemed to be paying attention to everything— the wind, a barn cat, shadows on the ground—everything except what Stevie was asking her to do. This is the calm, collected horse I rode in the Founders' Day Parade? Stevie asked herself. Belle, what's gotten into

17

you? Belle caught a glimpse of a passing truck and shied again.

Is my horse really this much worse than Phil's? No! Stevie wouldn't allow herself to think it. She would make Belle behave, perfectly, right now. She gave Belle a whack with her crop—it wouldn't hurt the horse, but it would certainly get Belle's attention. Belle bucked.

"Stevie Lake!" Max commanded. "Let's see a circle at the sitting trot."

Stevie sat deep in the saddle and used her weight and back to steady Belle's trot. She tightened her legs around Belle's sides and commanded her to circle. Belle turned, but she tossed her head. Stevie shortened the reins. Belle steadied her head but looked angry about it, and at the end of the circle she bucked again.

"Get it together, Stevie," said Max. "Soften her. Circle again."

Stevie tightened her grip on the reins. She would *make* Belle behave.

Across the ring, Carole recognized the look of grim determination on Stevie's face. She shot a worried glance to Lisa, who nodded miserably. Belle was in a temper, but so was Stevie. She and Lisa had seen Stevie look like this before, and the results were never good.

Belle bucked again. "You stupid horse!" yelled Stevie. She couldn't help it. Today, of all days, it seemed so important that Belle behave.

"Stevie, you know better than to act like this in one of my lessons," said Max, sounding truly outraged.

"Oooh," cooed Veronica diAngelo, whose horse, Garnet, had behaved impeccably the entire class, "is darling Stevie getting in trouble?"

"I'd say you know better than to act like that, too, Veronica, except that you probably don't," Max retorted. "I'd like to see some manners from all of you, starting *now*. Is that understood?"

"Yes, Max," they mumbled.

LISA THOUGHT IT was probably the worst riding lesson of her entire life. She was actually relieved when it was over. She dismounted Prancer and gave her a few tired pats.

"Wow," said Carole, riding Starlight up to Stevie and Lisa. "That was a mess, wasn't it? You both look like you've had rotten days. Why don't we all go to TD's—my treat. A Saddle Club special." TD's was an ice cream parlor near Pine Hollow that The Saddle Club frequented.

"Sounds fantastic," said Lisa wearily. "I'd really love it. Thank you, Carole." She ran Prancer's stirrups up and looped the reins over her arm.

19

Stevie, still in the saddle, looked grim. "Thanks, Carole. It sounds great, and I really would like to go, but I think I'd better work with Belle a little bit more."

Carole frowned. "Belle's had enough work for today, Stevie—don't you think?" Carole wasn't sure. Starlight almost never behaved as badly as Belle had.

"No," said Stevie. "She's not even trying to listen to me, Carole. I'm not going to make her canter or even trot—I'm not trying to wear her out—but I'm going to work her at the walk until she gives in and starts listening to me. She knows better than to act like this." At least, Stevie thought, I *hope* she knows better. She couldn't quite erase the doubt she was beginning to feel.

Lisa saw Carole start to say something to Stevie but then decide not to. Lisa understood. When Stevie was this upset, she rarely listened to advice—she would only get upset with Carole, too. And certainly riding Belle at a walk wasn't going to hurt her. Like Carole, Lisa wasn't sure what she would do if Belle were her horse.

Inside the barn, the first thing they heard was Max shouting again. "Can't you children keep yourselves under control?"

"Wow," muttered Lisa.

"I agree," said Carole. "This sure isn't the Max we know."

They walked their horses quietly down the aisle. Max was standing in the doorway of the tack room, scolding a group of younger riders inside. May Grover was staunchly defending herself and the others. "We were only playing tag in the tack room, Max, not in the stable. We know better. We weren't going to frighten the horses."

"You were making too much noise," Max told her. He dropped his hands from his hips and smiled, but the smile seemed forced. "Next time, make it silent tag, okay?"

"Okay." The little kids looked relieved.

Max turned and saw Lisa and Carole. He ran his fingers through his hair. "Nice job with Starlight today, Carole," he said. "You were the one highlight of that awful lesson. And Lisa, I'm sorry I yelled at you. I don't like you coming late, but what was it you said— dentist?—I guess you couldn't help that. I've just had one of those days."

"I know what you mean, Max. I've had one, too." Lisa felt much better.

As Lisa and Carole left to walk to TD's, they passed Stevie and Belle in the outdoor ring. Stevie was asking Belle to back up, halt, walk forward, halt, and back up again—simple exercises that Belle knew well and should have done easily. Belle was doing them, but Lisa could see that the mare wasn't happy about it. Her ears were back and her expression was mulish; clearly, she was still resisting Stevie.

"Poor Stevie," said Lisa, as they waved to Stevie and walked on. "I wish she had come with us."

"Poor Belle," added Carole. They waited for a car to pass and crossed the road.

"I agree," said Lisa. "Usually Belle seems so glad to do whatever Stevie asks. She seems so in tune with Stevie. I can't really believe this is all Belle's fault. I know she started out badly today—it certainly wasn't Stevie's fault that she shied at that newspaper, but still—"

"Right," said Carole with a nod. "When a horse misbehaves, you have to correct it, and all horses misbehave sometimes, but I'm not sure Stevie's correcting Belle the right way."

"Belle's a lot like Prancer," Lisa said. "They're both mares, and both are high-spirited and sensitive. I can't force Prancer into doing something she doesn't want to do—it's more like I have to convince her that she does want to do it. Belle's like that. I bet she's reacting to Stevie's bad mood as much as to anything else."

Carole sighed. "That's what's worrying me about this flying change scheme," she said, shaking her head.

22

"With horses, you can't put learning on a timetable. Some things take longer to teach than others. It's not really fair for Stevie to say that Belle has to learn flying changes in two weeks."

"We'll help her," Lisa reminded her friend.

Carole smiled ruefully. "It's just that right now we don't know how."

On Thursday afternoon, Carole arrived at Pine Hollow just as Lisa's mom was dropping her off. They greeted each other gladly. "This is beautiful weather," said Carole. "Let's go for a trail ride!"

"Fantastic!" Lisa agreed. Yesterday she'd had to go shopping with her mother and her aunt Phyllis, and she hadn't been able to come to Pine Hollow at all. This morning her mother had suggested that Lisa take a summer "cultural enrichment program," which consisted of classes in ballet, ballroom dancing, painting, and music appreciation. Lisa was fuming. She didn't want to appreciate music. All she wanted to do was

24

spend as much time around horses as possible. A trail ride was just what she needed.

Inside the barn, the first thing they noticed was Belle's empty stall. Red was giving a private lesson in the outdoor ring, and they knew Stevie wouldn't go out on the trails alone. They checked the indoor arena and found Stevie cantering Belle in figure eights. A pole was laid on the ground crosswise in the center of the eight. Both Stevie and Belle were sweating heavily in the hot, enclosed arena.

"Hi." Stevie greeted them glumly. "We don't have anything to show you, I'm afraid."

Carole leaned against the arena's gate. "I've seen that exercise in books," she said. "It's supposed to teach her a flying change, isn't it?" She explained to Lisa, "When you canter figure eights on the same lead, the horse is on the wrong lead half the time and should feel pretty unbalanced. Also, the horse will tend to jump the ground pole, and a flying change is easier for the horse to do out of a jumping motion. So the idea is that the horse will do a flying change over the ground pole in order to keep its balance during the second half of the figure eight. Isn't that right, Stevie?"

Stevie nodded miserably. "That's right. But it isn't working. We've been doing this for an hour, and not only has she not done a flying change, she hasn't done anything remotely resembling one."

Stevie used her shirt sleeve to mop the sweat from her forehead. "She doesn't jump the pole, she just canters over it, and she doesn't seem to mind turning on the wrong lead."

"I don't know," Carole said quietly. "I've never tried this exercise before." She wished she could help Stevie—usually she knew so much about horses that she had more advice than anyone wanted to hear, but today she had none. When she had gotten Starlight, he'd already known how to do flying changes, and all Carole had to do was work on refining them. But she didn't think it would help Stevie to hear that.

"We did this yesterday, too," Stevie said. "It wasn't any different." She sounded miserable even to herself. The worst part, she thought, was something she didn't even want to tell her friends. What if the trouble wasn't with Belle? What if the trouble was Stevie? What if she really wasn't a good enough rider to train her own horse? Stevie rarely talked about it, but she loved dressage, and sometimes she dreamed of riding in Grand Prix competitions. What if she wasn't good enough? This trouble with flying changes might be only the start.

"Come on a trail ride with us," Lisa urged. "We've hardly gotten a chance to see you. Belle looks tired.

26

Put her away and take Topside. Let's have some *fun*."
I really miss being with you, Lisa added to herself.

"Belle could have a nice time out in the back pas-
ture, and you could have a great time riding with us,"
Carole said. "You can't work this hard all the time."
She smiled encouragingly.

"Please, Stevie," Lisa said. "It didn't seem right at
TD's without you."

Stevie looked down at the smiling faces of her two
best friends. Part of her—a large part of her—wanted
to stay and ride Belle until Belle had done a flying
change, but another part of her thought maybe the
rest of The Saddle Club was right. She and Belle had
done enough work for one day. Maybe being with Lisa
and Carole would make her feel better about riding.

"Okay," Stevie said. "I'll hose Belle down and turn
her out in the pasture, and then I'll see if I can take
Topside. I'll meet you by the good-luck horseshoe, all
right?"

"Good," said Carole. As they walked away she
whispered to Lisa, "I don't remember ever having to
talk Stevie into a trail ride before."

"No," Lisa said. "Belle hasn't had any fun, either.
Stevie's ridden her hard for four straight days, and the
only thing they've done, aside from our lesson on
Tuesday, is work on that stupid flying change. Belle

hasn't had time to think about anything except hard work and flying changes."

"Belle looks miserable," said Carole. "It isn't that Stevie's really doing anything wrong—I know she would never hurt Belle—but I just don't think what she's doing is *right*." They paused in the tack room to gather their saddles and bridles.

"Stevie looks miserable, too," Lisa added. "She looks worse than she did on Tuesday. We need to do something to help her."

Carole paused in the act of taking Starlight's bridle off its peg. "Do you think Mrs. Reg could help?" she asked. "She knows practically everything about horses." Mrs. Reg, short for Regnery, was Max's mother and the stable manager. She was famous for her sometimes cryptic but always sound advice.

"It's certainly worth a try," Lisa said. They left their tack and hurried to the stable office. Mrs. Reg greeted them warmly.

"Here are two of my three favorite girls, The Saddle Club," she said. "Where's Stevie?"

"She's outside, cooling off Belle," said Lisa. "That's what we wanted to talk—"

The office door flew open and Max stormed inside. "That Patch!" he shouted. "Can you believe—he's gone and gotten an abscess in his hoof! He'll be lame for two weeks!" Max threw a towel onto the chair.

"Well," Mrs. Reg said mildly, "Patch did it on purpose, I'm sure, just to mess up your plans."

Carole and Lisa, who had been somewhat alarmed at Max's outburst, tried unsuccessfully to stifle giggles. Patch was a dear, quiet lesson horse. He almost never did anything wrong—and no horse would intentionally step on a nail and develop a painful abscess on purpose. It made as much sense as saying that Lisa would come down with chicken pox on purpose.

Max laughed, too. "I'm sorry, Mom," he said. "But really, it's quite inconvenient. I've got six beginners coming for a lesson in five minutes, and six more coming in an hour, and there aren't too many horses I trust with beginners as much as Patch." He rubbed his jaw. "Have you noticed, I seem to be apologizing a lot these days?" he added.

Mrs. Reg nodded. "This whole week," she said.

"It's just—I never get any peace and quiet around here," he said plaintively. "I don't think any of you realizes. London was my first week away from this stable in longer than I can remember, and it was peaceful —really relaxing. And of course Deborah was there, and now she's away—I'd just like a little peace and quiet, that's all, just a little."

"A little isn't too much to ask for," Mrs. Reg replied soothingly. "I'm sure we can find you some somewhere. And Deborah will be home soon."

"Not for another *week*," said Max, looking upset once again. He shrugged. "Call Judy Barker about Patch, will you, Mom? I'd better go tackle those beginners."

"I hope he doesn't scare them away," Mrs. Reg said thoughtfully, as Max closed the door.

"Is this what love does to people?" Lisa asked.

"Oh—sometimes. Didn't you girls have a question to ask me?"

"It's about Stevie," said Carole. "She's convinced that Belle has to learn flying changes right away."

"And why is that?" Mrs. Reg asked.

Carole and Lisa exchanged glances. Somehow it didn't seem right to explain about Stevie's competition with Phil. "She just does," Lisa said. "But she's entirely focused on it, and neither she nor Belle is having any fun. They aren't learning the changes, either."

Carole looked out the back window. "Stevie's just turned Belle out now," she said. "She'll be coming in to tack up Topside, if that's okay with you." She turned to Mrs. Reg. "We talked her into going on a trail ride with us," she said.

Mrs. Reg smiled. "Sounds like you two have the right idea," she said. "Why don't you go have a nice time, and do everything you can to encourage Stevie to have a nice time on Topside."

"Thank you," Carole said gratefully. "It's frustrating when you want to help, but don't know how."

"It's frustrating whenever you don't know how to do what you want to do," Mrs. Reg answered. "That's part of Stevie's problem, too, isn't it? Have a good ride, girls. I'd better call Judy about Patch." She turned to dial the vet's number.

THE TRAILS AROUND Pine Hollow were in full summer glory. Wildflowers dotted the woods on each side of the path, and birds and butterflies flew by them. Lisa took a deep breath of clean air and felt herself begin to relax. Her week hadn't been as difficult as Stevie's, but it had been hard enough. "This is great," she murmured. "Everyone should go on trail rides when they're upset. Think what it would do for the world."

"There wouldn't be enough horses," argued Stevie. "There wouldn't be enough trails. Think of all the stressed-out bureaucrats and executives in Washington, D.C., alone." Pine Hollow was close to the capital; sometimes a member of Congress or an ambassador came there to ride.

Carole bent to stroke Starlight's neck. "We're lucky."

Stevie grinned. "Yes, we are." For the first time in several days, she felt content.

* * *

THEY RODE FOR nearly an hour. On their way back to Pine Hollow, they stopped at their favorite rock by the stream, tethered the horses, and waded in the cool water. "I'm really glad you came with us, Stevie," Lisa said.

"So am I," Stevie replied, and they smiled at each other happily.

But when they left the woods, Stevie began to worry about flying changes again. Topside, her mount, was a former international-level show horse, and he'd done a lot of dressage. Before Stevie had gotten Belle, she'd ridden Topside almost exclusively. If any horse at Pine Hollow could do flying changes, Topside could.

"I'm going to canter," Stevie warned Carole and Lisa. She asked Topside for a right-lead canter. He took off willingly. A few paces down the path, she shifted her weight back in the saddle, tightened the left rein, and signaled with her right heel to ask for a left-lead canter. Without hesitation, Topside did a perfect flying change. Stevie repeated the request for a right-lead canter. Topside obligingly did a second flying change.

Stevie dropped him back to a walk. It was so easy for Topside! Why couldn't it be easy for Belle? She felt close to despair.

"That was fantastic!" Lisa came trotting up to her. "I saw those flying changes—I'm not sure I could ask a horse to do them right, but whatever you did sure made sense to Topside!"

"Of course it did!" Stevie cried bitterly. "He's a superstar horse. Dorothy DeSoto taught him all sorts of dressage movements. Of course Topside can do them!"

"Belle will be able to do flying changes, too," Carole said comfortingly, bringing Starlight up to join them. "Don't worry, Stevie, you know she can—almost all horses can learn them eventually. Belle's smart and athletic. Don't worry."

But maybe the problem wasn't Belle, Stevie thought. Maybe it was her—not the way she rode, but the way she trained her horse. Or maybe Belle really wasn't any good. Or maybe both.

"Don't worry," Lisa said, echoing Carole's words. She didn't really understand. She didn't worry about flying changes. She'd never even done one. Why should one little thing bother Stevie so much? It seemed to Lisa that the competition between Stevie and Phil had finally gotten completely out of hand.

In Topside's stall, Stevie gave the horse a pat on his shining flank. "Good boy," she murmured automatically. "Thank you for the nice ride." A sudden pang in her heart made her lean her head against his neck and shiver. She loved Belle so much; she loved Topside, too. What if Belle could never be the horse that Topside was? Would Stevie start to wish that she were still riding Topside? What if—

"Stevie," Mrs. Reg said from the aisle, "come out here when you're finished, please."

Stevie quickly patted Topside once more, checked his water bucket, and came into the aisle. Carole and

Lisa were already sitting side by side on a hay bale, looking up at Mrs. Reg expectantly.

Mrs. Reg smiled at them, and Stevie thought Lisa and Carole looked relieved. Stevie slouched against the wall. "You know," Mrs. Reg began, "for some reason this morning I started remembering my mare Madeleine. I rode her when I was not much older than the three of you."

Carole and Lisa smiled, and Stevie felt herself getting interested. Mrs. Reg's stories—though sometimes confusing—were always worth listening to.

"Maddy was a beautiful chestnut and the first Thoroughbred I ever owned," Mrs. Reg continued. Her face took on a faraway look. "She was a superb field hunter, born to go with the hounds—"

"Foxhunting," Carole mouthed, and Stevie nodded.

"—and she was a wonderful athlete, with a beautiful, stylish jump. But I admit, her personality could be difficult sometimes. She had a sense of humor, that horse." Mrs. Reg shook her head fondly.

"I'd been riding her about a year when our hunt held a hunter trials," she continued. "That's a horse show just for foxhunters, you know. Oh, I was certain that Maddy and I would win everything. I dreamed about blue ribbons every night."

Lisa smiled a little uncomfortably. She had been in that position before—she had taken Prancer to a show, certain they would win everything. Prancer had kicked a judge and been disqualified. The experience had taught Lisa to concentrate on riding well, not winning.

"The hunter trials course was in a big open field, with solid jumps—log fences and stone walls—typical of hunt country," said Mrs. Reg. "I schooled Maddy over it every single day for weeks before the trials. She started out well, but one day she began to refuse to jump, not for any reason that I could see. I got so mad at her—I wanted a ribbon!—but nothing I did helped." Mrs. Reg smiled and shook her head. "Such a fuss," she said. "But that was all a long time ago. Anyway, what I wanted to tell you girls—"

"But Mrs. Reg," Lisa cut in, "what happened at the hunter trials? Did you get a ribbon?"

"Well, of course not," Mrs. Reg replied. "We weren't eligible."

Carole frowned. "Not eligible? But you said—"

"Carole," Mrs. Reg said patiently, "you must know that no horse can receive a ribbon if it has been eliminated from the class."

"But that means—" said Carole.

"You can be eliminated in one of three ways: by your horse going up to a jump and refusing it three times, by falling off your horse, or by jumping the jumps in the wrong order. That last one," she said reflectively, "we didn't do."

"You mean you *fell off?*" Even though Stevie knew that all riders fell off their horses sometimes, she couldn't imagine it happening to Mrs. Reg.

"As a matter of fact, yes, I did," Mrs. Reg said crisply. "Maddy refused three fences in both of our first two classes, and in the third class she tossed me right over the log pile. Once I was on the ground I understood what my mistake had been." Mrs. Reg grinned at the recollection.

Stevie felt her throat tighten. "Your mistake was that you thought she was a good horse," she guessed. "You were wrong."

Mrs. Reg looked astonished. "Why, no. She was one of the best horses I ever had. Someday I'll show you a picture of us in full hunting regalia. But that is *not* why I wanted to talk to you girls. I just had a phone call from Dorothy and Nigel."

"Dorothy DeSoto and Nigel Hawthorne?" said Lisa. "Oh, wow! Are they coming to Pine Hollow?"

"Are they giving another dressage demonstration?" asked Carole. "Is Nigel going to be in a show? Is he competing for Great Britain again?"

"When do they get here?" asked Stevie. "How long can they stay? Do you think Dorothy will want to ride Topside? I can get him ready for her."

"No, no, no," said Mrs. Reg. "Dorothy and Nigel aren't coming here. They want you to go to them."

The Saddle Club screamed with delight. "Oh, wow! To visit their farm on Long Island! Only Carole's gotten to do that. Or wait—do they want us to come to New York City again?" All three of the girls talked at once. Carole and Lisa leaped up from the hay bale and exchanged hugs with Stevie.

Dorothy DeSoto and Nigel Hawthorne were good friends of theirs—The Saddle Club had even helped arrange their wedding. Dorothy was one of Max's old students and had been a top-level rider before an accident had taken her out of the show ring forever. Nigel, her husband, had ridden on the British Equestrian Team. Together they ran a show stable on Long Island, and Carole had once spent a few days with them there.

"You girls are beginning to frighten the horses with all this excitement," Mrs. Reg said. "Just like Max keeps telling you not to do. I think you'd better come along to my office, and I will explain things to you. Do not let your imaginations run wild. You aren't going to be able to guess this, anyway."

Carole, Lisa, and Stevie exchanged grins as they followed Mrs. Reg to the stable office. Everything they'd ever done concerning Dorothy and Nigel had been fun.

Mrs. Reg sat down in her leather chair and motioned the girls to sit, too. Carole perched on a window ledge, Lisa took the folding chair, and Stevie sat cross-legged on the floor. "Now try not to interrupt," Mrs. Reg said severely, but a smile twitched at the corners of her mouth. "You may not be that excited when I explain everything to you. Dorothy and Nigel need The Saddle Club's help."

"*They* need *our* help?" Lisa's voice squeaked.

"They can have it," Carole said. "Whatever it is."

Mrs. Reg nodded. "You remember Dorothy's mother, Mrs. DeSoto—"

"Well, of course," Lisa said indignantly. "We stayed at her townhouse in New York City, when we went to watch Dorothy ride at the American Horse Show."

"Right. Well, she hasn't sold her town house, but for a while she's been looking for a reason to get out of the city during the summer months. It's hot there, and a lot of people go to the shore. But Mrs. DeSoto likes to keep busy—she's not the type to sit around on a beach. Dorothy and Nigel have found the perfect solution. They just bought a Victorian house on Chincoteague Island. Mrs. DeSoto's going to run it as a bed-and-breakfast during the summer months.

"However, the house they bought needs a lot of fixing up before it can open for business. Dorothy and Nigel can't spend the entire summer working on it, and Mrs. DeSoto certainly can't do all the work herself. Plus, they really want the inn to be open for Pony Penning Week in early July, the busiest time of the year on Chincoteague. So what they've done is send out an all points bulletin to their old friends, asking for help. They'd like to get most of the work done next week.

"Denise McCaskill has asked if she could go," Mrs. Reg continued. "Red isn't going, because Pine Hollow can't spare him, but Denise said she'd really like a change of pace. Max was going to go, but"—Mrs. Reg's smile widened—"he just got an overseas phone call from Deborah. She's managed to cut short her commitments by almost a week, and she's coming home Sunday. Max said they would come to Chincoteague and work, but I thought since I'll be gone, they should stay and have the house to themselves for a few days. Max hasn't been quite himself lately." Mrs. Reg paused. "I guess Deborah's missed Max as much as Max has missed her," she said thoughtfully. "Otherwise, why would she be coming home early?"

"What about us?" asked Carole.

"Oh, right," said Mrs. Reg. "Well, of course, Dorothy and Nigel want you to come, too. In fact, Nigel specially asked for you—he said any trio that could arrange his wedding so well, and so quickly, would be just perfect for fixing up the inn! We'd leave early this Saturday—day after tomorrow—and come home next Friday morning. If we're successful maybe the inn will be ready for a few customers by next weekend. Dorothy and Nigel don't expect you to work twenty-four hours a day. The deal is this: You work four or five hours a day. In exchange, you get to spend a week in a Victorian mansion and enjoy the beautiful beaches of Chincoteague Island. Plus, of course, Dorothy and Nigel's company. What do you think?"

Lisa thought it sounded like just what she needed—a vacation! Stevie, frowning, picked at the heel of her boot, but Carole spoke first.

"You keep saying 'Chincoteague,'" she said to Mrs. Reg. "Do you mean *the* Chincoteague? As in *Misty of Chincoteague*?"

"I MEAN IT," Stevie said. "I really don't want to go."

"I can't believe you wouldn't want to go!" Lisa said. "This is Chincoteague Island, Stevie. Haven't you always wanted to see it?"

"Don't you remember the book?" Carole asked. "*Misty*? C'mon, Stevie!" Carole had called both Lisa and Stevie—three-way calling was a great invention as far as The Saddle Club was concerned—to discuss plans for their week on the coast. Stevie's attitude didn't make any sense to Carole—Marguerite Henry's *Misty of Chincoteague* had always been one of Carole's favorite books. Carole knew she'd gladly spend more than a week working for anyone, let alone good friends like Dorothy and Nigel, for a chance to see where the book actually took place. She could still remember the descriptions of Chincoteague Island and Assateague Island.

"Of course I read the book," Stevie said. "A zillion years ago, when I was a little kid. Of course I like it. That isn't the point."

"I read it again this afternoon," Carole said. "Right after Mrs. Reg asked us to go."

"That isn't the point," Stevie repeated.

"Didn't Mrs. Reg call your parents?" Lisa asked. "They'll let you go, won't they?"

"Yes, she called them." Stevie was beginning to feel exasperated. Why couldn't her friends understand? "My parents would be happy to have me gone for a week, believe me. But—"

"I'm amazed that you'd pass this up," Carole interrupted. "Think about it, Stevie—a free vacation *and* a chance to get away from your brothers. And it really doesn't sound like we'll have to do too much work—no more than what we would do at Pine Hollow anyway in the summertime."

"I'm not afraid of hard work," Stevie retorted. "You know that, Carole. In fact, that's why I don't want to go to Chincoteague. I want to stay here and work on

Belle. She's got to learn those flying changes. You and Lisa go. I'll be okay."

"But aren't you curious about Chincoteague? Don't you want to see it?" asked Lisa. "You remember Misty —the wild foal born on Assateague Island—remember, Stevie? How they swam her across the channel to auction her off?"

"But she was too little, and she almost drowned," Carole cut in. "That's my favorite part—Paul Beebe jumped in the water to save her. He swam her to shore."

"And Paul and his sister, Maureen, bought Misty and her mother, the wild Phantom," Lisa recalled. "And the book is dedicated to them and to other people from Chincoteague."

"They were all real people," said Carole. "That's my other favorite part. The wild ponies are real. They're still there today. Don't you want to see them, Stevie?"

Steve sighed into the phone. "It's not that I don't want to see them; of course I want to see them," she said. "And I'd love to go to Chincoteague with you, and see Dorothy and Nigel. But neither of you understands. I need to stay and work on Belle."

Carole thought that that just about summed up Stevie's problem—she wanted to "work on" Belle, not "work with" her. She wondered just how far Stevie would go not to be beaten by Phil. For Stevie's sake, as well as Belle's, Carole was determined to get her friend to Chincoteague Island. Stevie needed a break!

"You know, Stevie," she said slowly, "The Saddle Club is supposed to help whenever help is necessary. Dorothy's mother needs us. *All* of us are obligated to help her."

Stevie hesitated. "Mrs. DeSoto isn't part of The Saddle Club," she said at last. "The rule only says that you have to help Saddle Club members."

"Mrs. DeSoto let us stay in her house when we went to New York," Lisa reminded her, picking up immediately on Carole's argument. "She was very kind to us. This is our chance to pay her back. Plus, Stevie, this is also a way to help Max. If we all don't go, Max might feel like he and Deborah have to go. They won't get their chance to be alone together. Max might not be part of The Saddle Club, but The Saddle Club certainly couldn't exist without him."

"Exactly," Carole said.

"Lisa," protested Stevie, "you really don't think that Max would think he had to go, just because I didn't—"

"I certainly do."

There was a long pause on Stevie's end of the line. "All right," she said, giving in at last. "I'll go."

"Good," Carole said crisply. She had never imagined needing to talk Stevie into having fun!

45

*   *   *

THE NEXT AFTERNOON, Lisa ran into Carole at Willow Creek's shopping center. Carole was getting off a bus in full riding gear. She usually rode the bus to get to Pine Hollow, and the shopping center stop was the closest one to the stable. Lisa was wearing her riding clothes, too. They looked at each other and giggled.

"I suppose you're going to Pine Hollow," Lisa said, slipping her arm through Carole's.

"I suppose so," Carole agreed. "I suppose you are, too, since you usually don't shop in breeches and boots. I want to ride Starlight again before we leave. I'm really excited about this trip to Chincoteague— but I wish I could take Starlight with me!"

Lisa grinned. Today she had talked her mother out of the "summer enrichment" program—well, they had compromised. Lisa was going to take ballet again and possibly watercolor painting, but *not* ballroom dancing or music appreciation—and she had found her boot hooks in among her mane-braiding supplies, *and* she was about to leave for a week on a resort island with her two best friends! She could already feel the hot sand between her toes. Suddenly life was wonderful.

They walked along the road until they were within sight of Pine Hollow. Carole stopped. "Uh-oh," she said.

Lisa looked and stopped, too. She sighed. "Here we go again."

Stevie was riding Belle in the outdoor arena. Lisa was too far away to see exactly what they were doing, but she was sure it was another exercise designed to teach Belle a flying change. Stevie cantered Belle around a corner of the arena, then switched directions, throwing her weight around the corner. Belle chomped at the bit and swished her tail angrily. Instead of changing leads, she tossed her head and bucked. Stevie sat back and pulled Belle to a halt. Lisa was shocked at the expression on her friend's face—Stevie looked ready to cry.

Stevie spotted Lisa and Carole and rode Belle up to the rail.

"She won't do it," she said in an anguished voice. "No matter what, I can't teach her anything. This is a Bert de Némethy method—I got it out of his book on horse training—but I can't make it work! I'm not getting anywhere with Belle! She isn't any closer to doing a flying change than she was a week ago, and after we get back from Chincoteague I'll only have three days before I see Phil!"

Stevie sounded so upset that Lisa tried to think of a comforting thing to say. But before she could, Carole cut in.

"I've had it with you, Stevie Lake," she said sharply.

Lisa was amazed at the harshness in Carole's voice. Was Carole actually angry? At Stevie? Lisa couldn't remember when that had ever happened before.

"You're working that horse far too hard," Carole continued in the same angry tone. "It's not good for Belle. You'll end up actually hurting her if you keep at it like this. There's more to training a horse than making it do a flying change. You don't see me getting Starlight that upset, do you?"

Stevie's eyes blazed. "Well excuse me, Ms. Perfect Horsewoman," she replied. "But I am certainly not working my horse too hard. I do know *something* about training. Endurance riders cover a hundred miles of rough ground in a single day—I'm sure Belle can canter for half an hour without being hurt."

"Endurance riders don't do a hundred miles every single day," Carole spat back. "That's not the point, and you know it. Don't you remember Mrs. Reg's story?"

"Of course," Stevie said, tight-lipped. "She said Madeleine turned out to be a wonderful horse. So will Belle. Soon. Meanwhile, I think you should just—"

"Stevie, Carole!" Lisa was aghast. "Cut it out! This isn't helping!"

There was a long pause. "I guess you're right," Carole said slowly. "Stevie, I'm sorry. I didn't mean to yell at you." Carole paused. How could she explain how she felt, even to one of her best friends? "It's just that I don't really understand why this should be such a big deal to you, and I hate to see you and Belle getting so upset with each other. Usually you get along so well together. But I shouldn't have compared Belle to Starlight. I know that all horses learn things differently and have different personalities. I don't mean Belle should act like Starlight. I really am sorry."

"I'm sorry, too," Stevie said. She sighed and shrugged. "I didn't mean to lose my temper at you either. But this *is* important—and frustrating. Anyway, I need to ride Belle today, because I won't be able to ride her at all for a week."

"I thought the same thing about Starlight," Carole said. "Why don't you and Belle join us and Lisa on a trail ride? It'd be fun."

Stevie shook her head slowly but emphatically. "Not today. I really want to use this time for work, not fun," she said. "I'm sorry. I'd like to go with you."

"Okay," said Carole. "But I'm sorry, too. We'll miss you." She and Lisa went into the stable. "I really didn't mean to yell at her," Carole repeated.

"I know you didn't," Lisa comforted her. "But do you want to go on a trail ride without Stevie?"

"I guess so. It feels kind of strange—but it's her choice, Lisa. It's not like we don't want her to come."

Lisa quietly agreed and went to get Prancer's tack.

She couldn't help feeling that, even though everything in her own life was still going well, the day was not nearly as wonderful as it had been before she'd seen Stevie.

SATURDAY MORNING EVERYONE piled into Mrs. Reg's big station wagon. They threw their luggage into the back. Denise sat up front with Mrs. Reg, and The Saddle Club squeezed themselves into the middle seat. Lisa had brought her pillow in case she felt like taking a nap, and Carole had a tin full of her father's famous chocolate chip cookies. Stevie carried an armload of books.

"Stevie, don't tell me you're planning to study!" Carole said, laughing. "School's out, remember?" It was a well-known fact that Stevie rarely studied even when school was in. She opened her books whenever her parents threatened to limit her riding time until her grades improved—and even that didn't happen often.

"They're dressage books," Stevie explained defensively. "Training manuals."

"Oh." Carole shot Lisa a look, and Lisa rolled her eyes. They certainly weren't going to let Stevie spend the whole week reading about techniques to use on Belle!

Denise leaned over the back of her seat. "Are you

50

interested in training?" she asked Stevie eagerly. "Because if you are, I'd like to tell you about natural horsemanship. It's something I've been learning about recently at my college. It's a really great method of teaching your horse without using any force at all."

Stevie shrugged. "I don't use too much force," she said. Even to her, her words sounded a bit resentful. Denise was just trying to be helpful. But I've had it, Stevie thought. Everyone thinks they can tell me how to fix Belle—first Carole, now Denise. Pretty soon Dorothy's mother will be giving me advice, too.

Denise gave Stevie a sympathetic smile. "I'm sure you don't," she said. "I'll tell you about natural horsemanship some other time, if you're interested. Maybe I'll get a chance to show you what I mean. Demonstrations work better anyway."

Stevie read her textbooks throughout the drive through Washington, D.C., across the Chesapeake Bay Bridge, and down the Eastern Shore of Maryland back into Virginia. Once they were over the Bay Bridge, the scenery became somewhat monotonous—nothing but pine trees, cotton fields, and more pine trees—so Lisa taught Carole to play cribbage, and Denise and Mrs. Reg chattered gaily in the front seat.

Finally they entered Virginia's Eastern Shore, a thin strip of land that hung like an icicle off the east coast of Maryland. The narrow two-lane highway swung wide around a large, fenced complex, and the girls were surprised to see enormous satellite dishes and what looked like rockets standing on launching pads. "It's a NASA complex," Mrs. Reg explained, checking the directions Dorothy had given her. "Pay attention, now—we're almost there."

Just past the complex, a long skinny bridge led to Chincoteague Island. "This is funny," Carole said, frowning. "There wasn't a bridge in the books. They talked about taking boats to and from the mainland."

"It's new, I think, or a least a lot newer than the books," Denise said, looking over her shoulder at them. "There's a bridge from Chincoteague to Assateague Island now, too."

Carole wondered if she should feel disappointed. Part of her wanted everything about Chincoteague and Assateague to be just the way it was in the books —and part of her knew that bridges from the mainland to Chincoteague and from Chincoteague to Assateague certainly made it easier to visit the islands. She didn't know much about boats, and she doubted that Lisa or Stevie did either.

"There are certainly a lot of billboards," Lisa observed. "Look at that one, Carole! 'See the REAL Misty!' What do you suppose that means?"

52

"I don't know," Carole replied.

Stevie looked up from her books for the first time since they'd passed the Jefferson Memorial. "Humpf," she muttered, looking at the faded sign, "I bet the real Misty could do a flying change."

6

CHINCOTEAGUE ISLAND WAS beautiful. On the short drive to Mrs. DeSoto's new bed-and-breakfast, they caught a glimpse of the town. It wasn't old or new, fancy or plain; the shops and houses were a mixture of styles much as in the small towns of Maryland and Virginia they'd just driven through. But the island was beautiful—bright sunlight glinted off the bay, seagulls wheeled above them, crying loudly, and waves lapped softly against the piers. The air smelled salty and fresh.

"It's wonderful," Lisa said dreamily.

Mrs. Reg turned north on Main Street and stopped the car a few blocks later. "It certainly is," she said, looking up at the great white Victorian house in front of them. A white picket fence with peeling paint and a few missing slats encircled the yard. Roses ran wild across the top of the fence. The main house was three stories tall, with two chimneys, gable windows, a turreted side porch, and another wide porch running across the front. A brand-new clapboard sign read "The DeSoto Inn."

"Wow!" Even Stevie was impressed. They stared for a moment in silent admiration. Then the front door of the inn opened, and Dorothy and Nigel came running down the steps to meet them.

Dorothy greeted The Saddle Club with exuberant hugs. "It's been a long time since I've seen you," she said to Lisa, Carole, and Stevie. "Too long. You, too, Mrs. Reg—" and she hugged her as well, and then hugged Denise to round things off. The Saddle Club grinned. They had always liked Dorothy. At first they had mostly been impressed by her incredible riding skill, and then they had admired the courage with which she faced her career-ending back injury. Now they were just glad to have her as a friend.

Nigel shook hands all around, making funny little bows and saying "So good to see you." It was terribly British, and The Saddle Club loved it. Nigel was every bit as nice as Dorothy, but they couldn't imagine him hugging them.

Mrs. DeSoto appeared on the front porch. "Dorothy, don't leave them standing on the walk!" she called. "Bring them in! I've got scones just out of the oven!"

Mrs. Reg laughed and went inside while the girls, Denise, and Nigel carried the luggage up the front steps. Inside, the smell of fresh paint contrasted sharply with the wonderful fruity smell of hot scones.

"Sit down," Mrs. DeSoto said, herding them all into a dining room set with card tables and folding chairs. "I'm so glad to see all of you, and you're just in time. We're going to serve afternoon tea here at the DeSoto Inn, and Nigel's mum sent me her recipe for scones. You all can test them out." She disappeared through a swinging door and came back with a heavily laden tray. "Once you've had tea and rested, we'll show you the rest of the inn." She smiled. "We've been working hard—a few of the guest rooms are habitable, I'm sure you'll be glad to hear. And a few of the bathrooms and the kitchen are operational, too. But I'm eager to open for business. All of the other inns on the island are at full occupancy, or nearly so, and I want to start taking reservations for Pony Penning." She jumped up, went out to the kitchen, and came back with a small jar of jam. "I forgot—this is wild strawberry, in case anybody wants some. Now, what do you think of the scones?"

"Wunnerful," said Stevie, her mouth full.

"I agree," said Lisa. "I've had teas in England that weren't half so nice as this."

"Well, naturally," said Nigel, folding his legs and taking a close look at one of the currants on his scone. "Just because someplace invented something doesn't mean they've perfected it. I've also had some pretty grotty teas in England. I've made some pretty grotty tea, too, come to think of it—remember backstage at Olympia, luv?" He tapped his wife's cheek.

"Olympia is an indoor show in Great Britain," Dorothy explained to The Saddle Club. "It's right before Christmas, and it's a very big deal, kind of like our American Horse Show. Anyway, last year, Nigel was so nervous before the big Grand Prix that he insisted on making us all tea on a camp stove before the class got started. He said it would calm him down."

"Dreadful," said Nigel, with a shake of his head. "I boiled it, I'm afraid. Even my horse wouldn't drink it, and he loves tea."

"Did it calm you down?" asked Carole.

Nigel shook his head, a smile in his eyes. "Not at all. Nothing ever does, you know. But it didn't matter —I won the class anyway." He grinned.

"That's amazing," Stevie said frankly.

"What?" asked Nigel. "Amazing that I wrecked the tea? Or amazing that it didn't calm me down?" He raised his eyebrows at them in puzzled amusement.

"I agree," Carole said, and Lisa nodded.

"What?" Nigel repeated. "Do speak up. It's not like you Yanks to be uncommunicative—especially you three."

Stevie explained. "It's amazing that you were nervous before your class. I mean, you're *Nigel Hawthorne.* We didn't think great riders like you ever got nervous."

Nigel's grin widened. "Stevie, luv, have you seen Grand Prix jumps? They're six feet tall! Believe me, people who say they're not nervous before a class like that are flat-out lying—or shouldn't be there. You've got to care enough to be nervous, if you want to do well."

The Saddle Club nodded. Both Lisa and Carole felt somehow reassured—if even Nigel got nervous sometimes, then it was okay that they always felt a few butterflies in their stomachs before any kind of exhibition or show.

Stevie's line of thought was different. Immediately she tried to apply what Nigel had said to her situation with Belle. Did that mean it was okay that she was upset, because it meant she cared about Belle's doing well? At first Stevie felt better about herself. But then she realized that Nigel probably didn't get nervous when he was schooling his horses. He only gets nervous for shows—for big classes, she told herself, so should I be this upset with Belle, when Belle is just learning? But Belle wouldn't behave! She ought to be doing a flying change!

"Stevie," Carole said. "Come back. You're miles away."

Stevie blinked and smiled at her friend. "Sorry." She didn't explain what she was thinking about, and Carole didn't ask. From the anxious look on Stevie's face, Carole was pretty sure that Stevie had been worrying about Belle.

"Well," said Mrs. DeSoto, "judging by the way you all polished off those scones, I'd say the first tea at the DeSoto Inn has been a success. What you think, girls? Ready to see the rest of the inn?"

"We'll help you clean this up first," Lisa said quickly. She hadn't forgotten that the reason they were all there was to work. She picked up the teapot; Stevie stacked the empty dishes on the tray, and they all followed Mrs. DeSoto into the kitchen.

The big sunny room was their first surprise. The dining room still needed paint, wallpaper, and furniture, but the kitchen was completely done. It was wallpapered in a pale flowered print with a border of roses along the ceiling that complemented the roses on the fence outdoors. The white wooden floor shone. White chairs surrounded a big wooden table, and the institutional-size stove and refrigerator gleamed. The fence and a tangled garden were visible through a side window, and in the back a large plate glass window looked directly out onto the bay.

"Oh!" said Carole. "How beautiful!" She went to the window. A handful of fishing boats bobbed on the water, and birds skittered across the short strip of sand at the water's edge.

"Yes, we're directly on the bay," Mrs. DeSoto told her. "Only twenty inches above sea level. A little later you girls can go exploring. There's a more substantial beach in several places around the island—you can walk to lots of it. Chincoteague's only seven miles long, and a little over one mile wide at its widest."

Carole, Lisa, and Stevie stacked the dishes in the dishwasher and put away the butter and jam. Dorothy came in, followed by Denise and Mrs. Reg.

"Why don't I take you on the grand tour," Dorothy suggested. "I asked Nigel to take your suitcases up to your rooms. Fortunately, as Mom said, we do have three finished rooms. Eventually there will be seven—you can see how much work we still have to do."

Dorothy walked them back through the dining room, then showed them the sunroom and side porch. On the other side of the big staircase in the entryway was a room with a glass-fronted fireplace and rows of windows across the back. "This will be the parlor," Dorothy explained. "Mom's bought some real antiques and some new furniture that looks antique, and it will all be shipped just as soon as the rooms are ready."

Stevie scuffed at a pile of sawdust on the floor. "Looks like that might be a while. This room needs wallpaper, paint, and a good sweeping."

"You'd be surprised what a little hard work will do," Dorothy said. "Last week this room still had cobwebs, awful old wallpaper, a broken windowpane, and about seventeen coats of ugly varnish on that wood floor. There's still a lot of work to do, but it's coming along fast."

Dorothy led the girls to the small downstairs suite where Mrs. DeSoto would live. It was already clean and comfortable.

"It's pretty small compared to her town house in New York," Lisa said, looking around the two rooms. "Does your mother mind?"

Dorothy laughed. "I don't think so. She isn't selling the town house, Lisa. She's only going to run the inn between April and October. A lot of the businesses on Chincoteague close down for the winter—there aren't many tourists then."

Lisa nodded. She could see the attraction of spending part of each year in two such different places—so long as she could ride in both places. When The Saddle Club had visited New York, they'd ridden in Central Park. "Are there places to ride here?" she asked.

Dorothy shook her head. "Not lesson barns, no," she said. "Some of the people who live here ride, of course—they have to, at the Pony Penning Roundup. But I haven't seen or heard of a place yet where you can just go and ride. I'm sorry."

"That's okay," Lisa said.

Carole sighed. "Wouldn't a trail ride on Assateague be wonderful?" she said.

"Wonderful," said Dorothy. "But I don't think it would be allowed. I don't know for sure what the rule is, but I do know that you aren't allowed to bring pets onto Assateague. It's a wildlife refuge, and I think they're worried about pets bringing diseases into the wild population. I think horses would qualify as pets, in this case."

"Darn," Stevie said, and the others, including Denise and Dorothy, nodded. A trail ride on Assateague would have been fantastic.

On the second floor, there were five guest bedrooms, but only two contained furniture. "This is the room Nigel and I are using," Dorothy said, opening the door to reveal a four-poster bed, newly varnished wood floor, and stripped-down walls. "It's not quite done, but we thought we'd leave the finished rooms for you."

She walked across the hall and opened a second door. "This is the largest room at the inn, and when we're open it will be our finest. We finished it first, to inspire ourselves."

The visitors oohed and aahed. The corner room overlooked the bay and the garden. An enormous antique bed with an elaborate lace counterpane stood squarely between two lace-curtained windows. Opposite, a small fire was laid in a marble-fronted fireplace. An antique dresser, a spindle desk and chair, and a claw-foot bathtub in the private bathroom completed the furnishings.

"No TV," Denise noticed.

"No. Mom decided she wouldn't have any TVs in the entire inn," Dorothy explained. "Each room has a private phone, and we have heat and central air-conditioning, but that's as modern as she wants to get. No TVs, no VCRs, no faxes. This is a place for vacations."

"It's a beautiful room," Lisa said, examining the fine wallpaper and the rose rug in front of the fireplace. "It's for Mrs. Reg, of course."

"Of course," said Dorothy, smiling. "Nothing but the best for the first person to ever put me on a horse."

The third floor held two guest rooms that shared a single enormous bathroom between them. Denise's room was small and cozy, with a slanted ceiling and a double bed tucked under the eaves.

When they saw their room, The Saddle Club

couldn't help thinking that they'd gotten the best deal. The room had two gable windows with deep window seats giving them a beautiful view of the bay. A brass double bed took up the middle of the floor, and a matching daybed nestled between the window seats. The walls were covered with yellow-flowered paper, and the beds bore eyelet comforters.

Stevie sank down onto the big bed with a sigh. "This is fantastic," she said. "And to think I didn't want to come. And look, guys, Nigel brought my books up. Do you think I have time to read, or do you think Mrs. DeSoto needs us now?"

"I think she needs us," Carole said firmly. Lisa agreed. Wasn't anything going to take Stevie's mind off flying changes?

THEY HAD TIME to explore the sandy strip of beach before dinnertime. Then, at her insistence, Mrs. Reg treated all of them to a seafood dinner at a restaurant not far from the inn. Later that night they sat on the folding chairs in the dining room, and Dorothy and Nigel updated everyone on the training-and-breeding stable they were running on Long Island. All of them, including Denise, were fascinated by the couple's accounts of life on the show circuit. The Saddle Club went up to bed late, dazzled by the intelligent and powerful horses, the brightly lit arenas, and the wonderfully skilled riders who populated Dorothy and Nigel's stories. They fell asleep instantly and dreamed Olympian dreams.

The next morning The Saddle Club woke to the smell of hot cinnamon rolls. "Mom's working on her breakfast menus," Dorothy explained as the girls stumbled sleepily into the kitchen. "She'll have to serve breakfast every morning to the inn's customers."

"I'm practicing, same as with tea," Mrs. DeSoto told them. After her first bite of a spicy buttered cinnamon roll, Lisa raised her hand.

"I'll be a guinea pig," she volunteered. "Whenever you feel like practicing, call me!" The rest of The Saddle Club agreed.

They all accompanied Mrs. DeSoto, Dorothy, and Nigel to services at a small church on the island. Afterward they changed into shorts and T-shirts and met on the screened side porch.

"We're here to work," Stevie said. "What should we do first?"

Mrs. DeSoto and Mrs. Reg exchanged glances. "We've just been talking about that," Mrs. DeSoto said. "There are a lot of things that need doing, and we did ask you here to help us do them, but today I think we should all relax. The electricians are coming tomorrow to check the wiring, and a crew is going to start repairing the roof. Dorothy and Nigel will show you girls what they want you to do, but they've worked hard all week, and I think they should take a breather. Why don't we all take the rest of the day off and go at it strong tomorrow? Would that be okay?"

"Of course," Carole said.

"In that case," Denise suggested, "why don't I take the girls to Assateague?"

"HERE WE GO." Denise drove Mrs. Reg's car slowly across the bridge to Assateague Island. Carole, Stevie, and Lisa peered out the windows excitedly. A big wooden sign just over the bridge read Chincoteague National Wildlife Refuge, and the asphalt road stretched between tall stands of pine trees.

"Is this it?" Stevie asked. Somehow she had thought Assateague would look different from the rest of the coast. These pine woods looked very much like the woods around Pine Hollow. And she hadn't expected Assateague to have a real paved road.

"I know," Carole said, nodding. "It looks so normal."

"What did you expect?" Denise asked. "A whole herd of wild ponies standing by the bridge to greet you? Birds flying in formation overhead, and a big sign saying 'Here's to The Saddle Club'?" She smiled quickly at them, then checked the trail map Mrs. DeSoto had given her. "C'mon, guys, give the place a chance. We've only just gotten here."

Denise parked the car in a small lot near a brown building. "This is the Visitors' Center," she said. "Should we check it out first?" The girls shrugged and nodded. They followed Denise across the lot, looking around at the pine trees surrounding it.

"Where do you think the ponies are?" Lisa whispered to Carole and Stevie. Denise overheard her.

"Lisa!" she said. "Assateague is big—it's much bigger than Chincoteague, remember? The ponies are here somewhere. We'll see them!"

Carole nodded, her eyes taking on a dreamy look. "Assateague is the outrider island," she murmured. "It protects little Chincoteague from storms."

"What are you talking about?" Stevie asked her.

"I think it's a quote from that *Misty* book," Denise said. "Come on. Let's go inside." She herded them toward the door. Another sign read Chincoteague National Wildlife Refuge.

"Why is it called the Chincoteague Refuge?" Stevie asked, stopping. "Aren't we on Assateague?"

"I don't know," Denise replied. "I mean, yes, we're on Assateague; I don't know why it's called the Chincoteague Refuge. Maybe it's because part of Assateague is in Maryland, and that part isn't a refuge." She tapped Stevie's shoulder and motioned her forward. They went into the Visitors' Center.

Bright, life-size photographs of wild birds and animals and larger-than-life-size photographs of wildflowers hung on the walls. Otherwise the big room was plain and almost empty. A cheerful man in a park uniform greeted them. "Would you like some information on the wildlife refuge?" he asked. "I've got some pamphlets here on the types of plants and animals you could expect to see, and I can tell you which wildflowers are blooming now."

Denise went to pick up a few pamphlets. The Saddle Club looked at each other uncertainly. Finally Lisa spoke up. "We're mostly interested in the wild ponies," she said.

"Oh!" The man smiled. "Well, if you're here long enough, you should see them. The stallions hide their mares pretty well after Pony Penning, but that's still a month away. They aren't so cautious right now. Walk around the island. You'll find the ponies."

Denise thanked him and they walked back out to the parking lot. "There's a walking trail that starts right here," Denise said, pulling out Mrs. DeSoto's map. "Should we try it first?" The Saddle Club agreed.

They hadn't walked along the wide trail more than a minute before Stevie was no longer reminded of the Pine Hollow woods. Suddenly the trees grew sparse. The grass became long and luxurious, tall and thin, unlike the thicker meadow grass they were used to. Tiny blue flowers showed here and there. The ground underfoot felt spongy.

"It's marshland," Denise said. "The salt marsh." They continued walking. In front of them the land gave way to open water, sunk down in the marsh grasses, as far across as they could see. Herons wheeled above it.

"Is this the ocean?" Lisa frowned. She could see land in front of her again, on the other side of the water, but there was nothing but water stretching to either side. There were no other people in sight. They were alone with the flowers and birds. "It's wild," she said.

"Exactly." Carole sounded entirely satisfied.

Denise checked her map. " 'Snow Goose Pool,' " she read. "I don't know if it's freshwater or salt. And the way the edge just fades into muddy reeds, I'm not sure I want to get close enough to find out. But it looks like we can walk closer in if we go this way a little bit."

They followed her obediently to where a slender walking path branched off the main trail. They walked down the path among the marsh grasses. Carole felt as if she wanted to sit down so that the grass would hide her, then let the wildlife come as close to her as they dared. The blue sky was huge, and the grass smelled wonderful. This was exactly the way she had imagined Assateague would be. If a wild pony came galloping along the edge of that pool, she thought, this would be the best spot in the world.

They still couldn't get close to the water without sinking up to their knees in mud, but Stevie bent down and touched her finger to a puddle. "It tastes a little bit salty," she announced. "Not like the ocean, though." She made a face. "Mostly it tastes muddy."

Denise laughed but suggested they go see the ocean, and save further exploration of the Snow Goose Pool for later. "I'm really anxious to see it," she explained. "It feels so strange here. I know we're on an island, and we're surrounded by water all the time, but so far we've always seen land on the other side. I want to see waves."

The Saddle Club agreed. On the way back to the car, on the edge of the pine trees, they came across a group of miniature brown deer. "Oh, look!" Carole whispered. "Are they babies?"

"No," Stevie said, "because that one's got a baby—

see?" A tiny fawn stood close to one of the does. The deer watched them curiously.

Denise consulted one of her pamphlets. "They're Sika deer," she said. "They were brought here in the 1920s, and they like to eat the salt grass."

Carole moved slowly toward them, holding out her hand. "Do you think I can pet one?" she asked.

"I wouldn't try," Denise advised. "They might let you—they know they're safe on a wildlife refuge, and I'm sure they're used to seeing people. But they're still wild, and it's better if they stay that way."

Carole dropped her hand. What Denise said made sense. But she couldn't help wondering if the deer felt as velvety as they looked.

"Did you see the sign on the road?" Denise asked them. " 'Wild ponies kick and bite!' "

Carole smiled. "I didn't see the sign," she said. "But I knew that anyway."

BACK IN THE car Lisa asked suddenly, "Do you think it's true about the wild ponies?"

"What's true?" asked Stevie.

"All that stuff about them being on a Spanish ship, a galleon, and the ship getting wrecked on the coast, and the ponies swimming to shore?" Lisa said.

"Of course," Carole answered promptly.

"No," Stevie said, just as promptly. "It's a nice story

72

—but I don't think there were too many Spanish ships off the coast of New England."

"Sure there were," Lisa argued. "But what I mean is—"

"Wait a minute," Denise interrupted. "I know what you're asking, Lisa, and I don't think anyone knows the answer for sure. I was reading a book on local history that I found in my bedroom—kind of touristy but mostly facts, you know? It said that there are two versions of the ponies' origin. One is what you said. A ship—presumably a Spanish ship since the Spanish explorers are the ones who reintroduced horses to North America—wrecked and the ponies did swim to shore. That could have happened—there were a lot of shipwrecks recorded off the coast of Assateague once the settlers got here.

"But the second version is much simpler. European settlers started living on Chincoteague in the 1670s, and at first most of them were farmers. Some of them pastured their excess stock on Assateague. Some of the colonists' horses escaped and formed their own wild bands. The one thing we know for sure is that there have been wild ponies on Assateague for a long, long time."

The Saddle Club was silent for a moment. Denise started the car and began to drive toward the beach.

There was more traffic now—apparently the beach was a popular place.

"I like the Spanish wreck story better," Carole said at last.

"When did they start selling the ponies?" Stevie asked. "Did your book say that, Denise?"

Denise nodded. "Let's see—back in the 1920s, I think. They had a big fire on Chincoteague, and a lot of the buildings were destroyed. They didn't have the bridge to the mainland then, so they couldn't get a fire engine over, and they didn't have one on the island. Afterwards, the town had a big carnival to raise money for a fire engine. The first Pony Penning happened then. Part of Assateague Island goes into Maryland, like I told you before, and they've got a fence at the state border so the Maryland ponies don't get mixed up with the Virginia ponies. The Chincoteague Fire Department is responsible for taking care of the Virginia ponies."

"Mrs. DeSoto told me that selling the ponies is a good thing," said Carole. "It keeps the island from becoming overpopulated. If there were too many ponies, they might not have enough food."

They were driving along the edge of more pine woods. The tail of Snow Goose Pool appeared on their left. "Hey!" said Stevie. "There's a trail with a pony on it!"

74

Denise stopped the car. "A real pony?"

"No." Stevie looked embarrassed. "I mean—see that sign at the start of the trail? It has a pony on it, just like the marsh trail sign had a goose."

"Maybe there are ponies on the trail." Carole looked hopeful.

"Maybe." Denise sighed. "Look, I know you all want to look for ponies, but please, I want to see the ocean. Can't we do that first?"

"Sure," Stevie said, after a moment's hesitation. "Maybe there will be wild ponies on the beach."

THE ODDS OF the wild ponies' being anywhere on this beach, Carole reflected, were pretty small. The wide strip of white sand went for miles in both directions, but near the parking lot it was covered with people, lying on beach towels and wading in the surf, just like every other beach she had ever seen. Here was Denise's ocean, immense, unending, sending gentle waves against the shore. Carole took a deep breath of the clean ocean air. It was pretty wonderful, even without the ponies.

They left their shoes in the car and walked along the edge of the water, letting the waves slosh around their ankles. They walked for a long time, past the sunbathers and the children playing Frisbee, north to where Snow Goose Pool and the ocean almost con-

75

nected. Again they saw birds of all types. Suddenly Stevie stopped and looked down at the sand by her feet.

"I could be wrong," she announced, with a typical Stevie grin on her face. "But I don't think I am. Here's the first proof that there really are wild ponies on this island!"

Carole and Lisa looked. "Hoofprints!"

"Lots of hoofprints," Denise added. They searched the marshland and beach with their eyes, but they didn't see any ponies. "Maybe they come down here at night and play in the surf," Denise suggested.

"Surf ponies!" Stevie said. "They bring their beach towels and lie on the sand, and the foals go swimming, but not too far out—"

"You're far out," Carole put in. "Surf ponies! Everyone knows you wouldn't call them that. They'd be sea horses!"

They giggled. Lisa threw herself down on the sand, imitating a mare lying on a beach towel, and Stevie pretended she was a foal that had never seen the ocean before. She darted forward and back at the water's edge, rolled her eyes and pawed the sand, and looked so much like Samson, the colt at Pine Hollow, that The Saddle Club rolled on the sand with laughter.

"I hate to say this," Lisa said at last, checking her

watch, "but shouldn't we be thinking about heading back? It's going to take us over half an hour just to get back to the car, and we promised Mrs. DeSoto we'd help with dinner."

But we haven't seen the ponies yet, Carole felt like arguing. Still, she knew Lisa was right. They turned and began the long walk back to the car.

"We'll come back tomorrow," Denise promised them. "Thank you for letting me spend so long on the beach."

As THEY WERE passing the edge of Snow Goose Pond on their way back toward Chincoteague, they saw two things. First, standing on one foot in the water at the edge of the pond, was a huge bird with blue-gray feathers and a wise expression. A large crowd of people had gathered around him, some of them taking his picture. The bird seemed to regard all the attention with benevolent acceptance, Lisa thought, rather like a king receiving adulation from his subjects.

Denise slowed so they could get a closer look. "That's a great blue heron," she said. "I've never seen one. They're endangered, you know." She drove on past the Visitors' Center toward the bridge to Chincoteague.

"Wait!" cried Stevie. "Stop the car!"

"What's wrong?" Denise hit the brakes, and the car screeched to a halt.

"There!" Stevie pointed. "I think we scared them." They looked. Something was moving among the pine trees—a large something—many somethings—a pinto something?

"The ponies!" cried Carole. Sure enough, it was a band of wild ponies. The Saddle Club could see long manes and scruffy tails, darting glimpses of piebald and skewbald flanks, and the tiny movements of foals running close against their mothers.

"We scared them," Stevie repeated. "I think the car scared them."

"Ohh." Carole let out her breath with a rush of pent-up excitement. "At least we saw them. Now we know they're real."

Stevie gave her a strange look. "You knew they were real," she said.

"I knew," Carole said simply, leaning back against her seat, "but I didn't *know* until I saw them for myself."

"STEVIE? YOU'RE COMING with us, aren't you?"

Stevie let the dressage book slide out of her hands and land on the floor with a thump.

Lisa stood in the doorway of their bedroom, hands on her hips. "I thought you just came up to get your tennis shoes," she said.

Stevie shrugged and gestured toward the book. "I saw this lying here, and I just thought I'd look at it for a minute," she said. "Sorry if I kept you waiting."

"That's okay." Lisa looked around the room. Bright sunlight streamed in the open windows, and the ocean breeze pulled at the curtains. Outside, sailboats swept across the bay. It wasn't like Stevie to read a book on a day like today, especially now, when Denise was taking them back to Assateague. Lisa could tell that Stevie was still upset about Belle.

"You should try to just enjoy yourself this week," she told her friend as they hurried to meet Denise and Carole. They'd worked hard all morning, sweeping the dirt out of the parlor and priming the walls to be painted. "We're supposed to be having fun."

Stevie groaned. "Last night I dreamed that all the wild ponies on Assateague were doing flying changes," she said. "I'm trying to have fun, Lisa, but it hasn't been easy. There has to be some way to teach Belle!"

They had reached the front porch, and Stevie saw Denise's face light up with interest when she heard Stevie's words. Stevie shut her lips tight and wished she hadn't said anything about Belle. It was bad enough that her best friends in The Saddle Club didn't really understand. Carole had even criticized her! Stevie didn't feel like talking to Denise about it.

"You know," Denise said, as they drove through town and down the main road toward Assateague, "if you're interested in horse training, Stevie, I'd really like to tell you about natural horsemanship."

There was silence. Stevie, hunched in the backseat, didn't say a word. "We're all interested in horse training," Lisa said politely. "But I've never heard of natural horsemanship."

"That's because it's still pretty new," Denise explained. "It's a system for training horses that doesn't involve any force at all—I think I told you that. What you want to be able to do is get the horse to move in any direction you want, as fast or slow as you want, without force and with hardly any cues. Like, Carole, how do you get your horse to back up when he's on cross-ties?"

Carole thought. "I usually push on his chest and say 'Starlight, back up.' "

"Right," said Denise. "That's the way most people would do it. But with natural horsemanship, you could teach a horse to back up whenever you wiggled a finger back and forth under his nose. He'd back up without your even touching him."

"But my pushing on Starlight's chest isn't hurting him," Carole said. "I don't push very hard."

"Oh, no, that's just one example," Denise said. "Natural horsemanship is a whole system for ground training and teaching horses to go under saddle. It isn't really a riding system—it's more like a way to get a horse to listen to you and respect you, and obey you without ever being afraid of what you asked it to do. Both English and Western riders use it. For example, another thing I could do with a horse under this system is get it to walk straight into a horse trailer on a voice command."

Lisa leaned forward, interested. "You mean you could just tell it to get in the trailer, and it would?"

"Once I'd trained it, sure. It would just walk right in."

"Wow." Lisa could see the value in that. Some horses hated horse trailers. She could remember several times when one or another of the Pine Hollow horses had refused to load. After urging it forward and offering bribes of oats and carrots, Max and Red would occasionally have to resort to running a long lead rope behind the horse's rear and trying to pull it on board. Sometimes the horse would fight for half an hour. "Wouldn't that be great, Stevie?" she said. "Think how much more quickly we could get to horse shows if the horses all loaded that easily."

"Sure." Stevie didn't sound interested at all. "What part of the island are we going to see today?"

Denise glanced at Stevie. "I thought maybe the trail you saw with the pony sign on it," she said. "Dorothy told me this morning that there really are a lot of ponies near there. I know how much you all want to see them."

She parked the car on the side of the road near the trail marker and carefully locked the doors. "So a pony doesn't break in," she said, laughing, "or maybe yesterday's heron."

"He looks like he could pick a lock with his beak," Lisa agreed. "Tell us more about natural horsemanship, Denise. It sounds interesting."

"Well," said Denise, "if you wanted to start working with your horse this way, one of the first things you would do is start to touch it very lightly, all over its body. Most horses have a few sensitive areas—some don't like to have their mouths handled; others don't want you to touch their ears, or the tops of their tails, or the insides of their legs. So what you do is gently rub the horse, finding out where its sensitive areas are and moving very lightly over them at first. You teach it to trust you and also to allow you to handle it. And since most horses really enjoy being rubbed, overall it's a pretty positive experience for them."

"Prancer loves to be groomed, so I know she likes to be touched," said Lisa. "But she absolutely hates having her mouth handled. I always wondered if it was because they tattooed the inside of her lip with an identification number when she was on the racetrack. Anyway, whenever Judy comes to check her teeth we have to tranquilize her." Horses needed to have their teeth checked at least once a year.

"Exactly," said Denise. "So if, very gradually, you worked at handling Prancer's mouth, and you always backed away whenever she started to fuss and never tried to force her, she might learn that you weren't going to hurt her. She might learn not to be afraid of having her teeth checked, and maybe you wouldn't have to tranquilize her anymore."

"It's worth a try," said Lisa. "It's pretty traumatic for her the way things are now."

"Traumatic for both her and Judy Barker," confirmed Carole. "Prancer really puts up an argument."

"You know, I just don't agree with this," Stevie broke in. "Max always taught us to correct a horse whenever it misbehaved, to remind it to pay attention to the rider's instructions. Horses are taught to respond to a crop or a firm voice command. Max is a super horseman, and he's certainly not abusive. His way seems fine to me."

They rounded a bend in the trail, and Carole suddenly held up her hand, her eyes shining. "Look!" she whispered. At the far edge of an open field in front of them, a band of wild ponies grazed. The piebald stallion regarded them warily, but the mares didn't stir. Foals grazed beside nearly every mare.

"How beautiful!" said Denise. "Let's stand here a minute so we don't frighten them." She turned to Stevie. "I do understand what you're saying," she said. "And you're right, Max is a wonderful horseman. He never abuses his animals, and anything he teaches you will be sound. His methods are good, accepted, and appropriate.

"But Stevie, there are different ways to teach and learn just about everything. The method I'm talking about—natural horsemanship—is really only a slight variation on what Max is teaching you, but it's a variation I really like.

"The other important thing to remember is that there is a big difference between disciplining a horse that already knows correct behavior and trying to teach a horse correct behavior in the first place. I think natural horsemanship is an easier way to train horses—easier on the horse and easier on you."

Denise looked at the wild herd thoughtfully. "I know I shouldn't do this," she said. "But let me try to show you what I mean." She began to walk very slowly toward the nearest pony, a dark bay mare grazing a bit apart from the rest of the herd. Ever so slowly, The Saddle Club followed.

The stallion shifted his weight back and forth a few times before deciding that these strangers didn't pose a threat to his mares. He dropped his head and began to eat. A ripple of relaxation went through the band, and they allowed the girls to come close.

"Easy," Denise murmured to the bay mare. She moved slowly up to the horse's shoulder. "Good girl." Denise held her hand out for the horse to sniff, then carefully brought it up and began to rub the pony on its forehead. The mare looked surprised, but not alarmed. "Good girl," Denise repeated.

She brought her hand over the pony's poll, the area between its ears, and began to rub its neck as well, down the underside and then under the thick, rough mane. With her other hand she began to stroke its withers and back. The mare turned her head and blew out thoughtfully.

"She isn't frightened," Carole whispered. "She doesn't seem wild at all."

"Exactly," whispered Denise, a note of triumph in her voice. She moved her hand down the mare's flank. The mare shuddered and stepped away. "Easy, good girl." Denise returned to rubbing the mare's forehead, withers, and neck—all places she obviously enjoyed.

"Let me try," Carole said. Imitating Denise, she held her hand beneath the mare's nose and then began to rub its forehead. "She does like it! Lisa—"

Lisa rubbed the mare's forehead, too. She looked over at Stevie, but Stevie shook her head. Clearly Stevie still wasn't impressed by natural horsemanship.

"I'll show you something else," Denise said softly. "A really easy way to get a horse to pick up its feet is by squeezing its chestnuts. Watch." She gently ran her hand down the mare's leg and squeezed on the little patch of hairless skin that all horses have on the insides of their legs. The mare lifted her foot.

"Good girl!" Denise praised the mare. "And see, she's probably never picked up her foot on command before," she told The Saddle Club. "Let's try it with a back leg." She repeated her gentle squeeze. The mare hesitated, putting back her ears and tensing her haunches. Denise immediately let go of her leg and rubbed her neck some more. "You're okay, good girl."

"This is silly," Stevie said. "I know how to pick up a horse's foot. You do it like this." She put her shoulder against the mare's hip, ran her hand softly down the mare's back leg, and pulled up on her foot. The mare lifted her hoof a few inches from the ground, then waved her leg wildly, trying to get away.

Stevie held on. Whenever a horse—Belle, Topside, or any of the other Pine Hollow horses—tried to pull its foot, the person was supposed to hold on, she knew. The horse was just misbehaving.

The mare squealed in panic. She kicked Stevie sharply in the leg, wheeled around, and ran for the woods. The rest of the band, frightened, followed her. The herd disappeared with a thundering of hoofbeats, and the only sound in the clearing was Stevie crying out in pain as she clutched her leg.

THEY CLUSTERED AROUND her. Stevie was holding her upper thigh, grimacing, and blinking back tears. Without a word, Denise gently pried Stevie's hands away from her leg. She pushed Stevie's long khaki shorts up a few inches. Blood oozed from a few scratches surrounding a reddened, hoof-shaped welt.

"I'll be okay," Stevie gasped. "It hurts less already."

"Are you sure?" Carole asked anxiously. She had sprained her ankle once and had tried to pretend it wasn't hurt. She didn't want Stevie doing the same thing.

"I'm sure," Stevie said. "Her hoof must have been

pretty rough to scrape my skin like that, but at least she wasn't wearing shoes." They all nodded. They knew that a horse wearing steel shoes could do a lot more damage with its hooves than one that wasn't. "So I'll get a little bruise," said Stevie, trying to laugh. "It won't be the first time."

Denise shook her head. "Stevie, I am so sorry. This was all my fault. And me an A-rated Pony Clubber! I should have known better than to bring you so close to the wild ponies. I knew they were wild—I wasn't mistaking them for house pets. I'm really sorry."

Stevie shook her head. "You shouldn't be," she said. "I should have known better, too. I knew they were wild just as much as you did." She looked around at her friends. "Besides," she admitted, "I think we all wanted to touch a wild pony. I think I would have tried to ride one if I thought I could get away with it."

Her friends nodded. "It was really stupid of us," Lisa said. "I'm just glad you weren't seriously hurt."

Denise smiled ruefully. "That's what comes from being horse crazy, I guess. I'm just as bad as the three of you, even if I am older. Sometimes horse crazy turns out to be just plain crazy."

"Do you think you can walk back to the car?" Lisa asked. "Otherwise, we can go ask the park rangers for help."

"I can definitely walk," Stevie assured her. "And

please, don't anybody tell Mrs. Reg or Dorothy or Nigel about this. I don't want them to know how stupid I was."

Limping back along the woodland trail, Stevie reflected that she had indeed been pretty stupid. In fact, the more she thought about it, the more she was convinced that the accident had been entirely her own fault—after all, the pony hadn't kicked Denise. Stevie remembered how Denise had backed off whenever she did anything to make the pony uneasy, whereas Stevie had simply barged ahead and tried to force the pony do what she wanted.

She knew that there was absolutely nothing wrong with the way she had asked the pony to pick up its foot. And there was nothing wrong with the way she had hung on to its foot, either—nothing wrong, that is, if the pony had been trained to understand what Stevie was doing. As it was, the pony hadn't understood, and it had reacted with fear. Kicking, Stevie knew, was one of the pony's ways of defending itself.

The worst part, thought Stevie, was that she had *known* that the wild pony didn't understand what she was doing, but she hadn't changed her own behavior to help the pony understand. "I should have known better," she muttered.

Lisa turned. "What? Is your leg hurting?"

Stevie managed a small smile. "No. It's my brain that hurts—you see, I'm thinking, for a change."

THE NEXT DAY it rained, a steady, cold, soaking rain. Sailboats bobbed in the bay with their sails furled, and the tourist traffic on the island was noticeably thinner. All morning The Saddle Club repainted the parlor a delicate shade of shell pink. Lisa and Carole worked with rollers on the walls, and Stevie painted the trim with a small brush. First, however, Stevie outlined a life-size pink horse on one of the bare walls.

"Stevie!" Lisa said, turning just as Stevie was painting in a wind-tossed mane.

"You're going to paint this wall with the same paint anyway," Stevie said quickly. "I don't think the horse will show."

"But I didn't know you could paint horses!" Lisa said.

Carole burst out laughing. "Sure you did, Lisa. Don't you remember when we painted the barn?"

Lisa and Stevie started laughing, too. One of Pine Hollow's horses had gotten loose and run underneath their ladder, and a bucket of paint had spilled on him. He hadn't been hurt, but he had looked unusually colorful for a few weeks.

"Still," Lisa said, "you ought to be taking painting

91

classes this summer, not me. I'm going to tell my mom."

Stevie shook her head. "I only do horses," she said quickly. She stepped back to admire her work. "This is great, to have a whole wall to work on. Usually I've only got the margins of my math papers. Do you think it looks like Belle?"

Carole studied the painted horse's happy expression. "Yes," she said. "But I don't think you could draw a horse that didn't look like Belle. You know her best, after all."

A FEW HOURS later, when Mrs. DeSoto came in, Carole and Lisa were finishing their second-to-last wall, and Stevie had done almost all the trim. Mrs. DeSoto appeared at the door. "Flying change?" she read in a puzzled voice.

Lisa and Carole turned to her in equal puzzlement. Stevie looked slightly embarrassed. "There." Mrs. DeSoto pointed to the last wall—the one with Stevie's horse on it. Sometime after they had all started working, Stevie had gone back to her painting of Belle and added an arrow pointing to Belle's legs along with the words "flying change!"

"Oh that," Stevie said vaguely. "It's a thing a horse does—or doesn't, depending on the horse."

"Yes, I know," Mrs. DeSoto said. "I just wondered why you painted it on the wall."

"We saved that wall for last," Lisa chimed in quickly, sensing Stevie's discomfort, "because we really loved Stevie's picture. Isn't it a beautiful horse?"

"It is," Mrs. DeSoto agreed. "I'd even like to leave it there—but I think plain walls might go better with the curtains and furniture I've ordered. I came to tell you that I've made some hot soup for lunch, since it's such a cold day—homemade New England clam chowder, a specialty of the DeSoto Inn."

They laughed. All week long Mrs. DeSoto had been experimenting with new recipes, calling each one "a specialty of the inn."

"Lunch will be ready soon," she concluded. "As soon as you're finished painting, come eat!"

AFTER LUNCH THE girls sat in the bright kitchen and looked out the windows. The rain showed no signs of stopping. "I don't think today is a good day for Assateague," Denise said.

"I agree," Stevie said. "The marshlands are wet enough in dry weather. Today we'd sink in up to our knees!" Stevie's thigh felt stiff and sore, and she was glad to have an excuse not to walk much.

"There's always the beach," Denise said, but even she sounded doubtful.

"No thanks," said Lisa. "Can you imagine how cold the ocean would feel today? *Brr!*"

Carole fingered the tablecloth reluctantly. "I've been trying to decide how I feel about this," she said. "I read that, somewhere in town here, they have Misty —I mean the real Misty, the pony—in a museum. We could go there." She looked up at her friends. "I'm just not sure that I want to."

Stevie frowned. "I know Misty was a real pony," she said. "But Carole—that book was written fifty years ago! Misty's dead!"

"Is that true?" Lisa asked.

Mrs. DeSoto nodded. "I have to know all about the island if I'm going to be a good innkeeper," she said. "Both Carole and Stevie are right. Misty had a good life; she lived to be more than thirty years old. When she died they stuffed her, like—I don't know, like a wildlife exhibit—and they have her in a little museum in town. I haven't been there, but I can tell you girls where it is."

"Eew," said Stevie. "I mean—I'm glad Misty was real, and I'm glad she had a good life, but I don't know if that means I want to see her skin."

"I'm with you, Stevie," Nigel said, toasting her with his cup of tea.

"I don't know," said Dorothy. "I've talked to some of the people in town, and one woman told me that it

94

seems to mean a lot to some children to be able to touch and pet Misty. It makes her more real to them.

"Paul Beebe was killed in a car accident when he was a young man," she continued. "Maureen is married and still lives nearby, but she's not the young girl she was in the book. A group of people are trying to raise money to buy Grandpa Beebe's house and set it up as a memorial, but his Pony Farm is already gone. Misty's the only thing that's still the same."

"That's not quite right," Denise argued. "The wild ponies are still the same, too. I mean, I read the book *Misty* when I was in the fourth grade and I really liked it. I guess I still do, but I think the live ponies on Assateague are the best memorial to Misty."

"You can touch them," Stevie muttered, rubbing the leg of her blue jeans, "and know they're real." Her friends gave her cautious looks. "I don't mean really," she added hastily.

"I guess, after all, I'd rather remember Misty the way she is in Marguerite Henry's book," said Carole. "I really don't want to see her." No one could argue with that.

"We could take a walk," Lisa suggested after a pause. "We haven't seen too much of the actual town yet."

"In this rain?" protested Stevie. "We'd freeze to death! No thank you."

Lisa remembered Stevie's bruised leg. She nodded understandingly.

"Well," Mrs. DeSoto said briskly. "I don't think we need to fill the house with any more paint fumes, not on a day when we can't possibly open the windows. I'll tell you what. I've got a great DeSoto Inn chocolate chip cookie recipe that needs testing. If you girls wouldn't mind—"

Stevie leaped up from the table so fast her leg started to throb. "Lead me to the chips!" she proclaimed.

Lisa and Carole grinned. This seemed like the Stevie they knew best and hadn't seen since the trouble with Belle began. Maybe Chincoteague was indeed just what Stevie needed.

NIGEL, DOROTHY, MRS. DeSoto, Mrs. Reg, and Denise all sat around the big kitchen table while The Saddle Club whipped up a super batch of cookies. Nigel made another pot of tea; Mrs. Reg made coffee, and they ate cookies and talked.

"I remember the first time you stopped me after one of Dorothy's riding lessons," Mrs. DeSoto said to Mrs. Reg, "and told me that you thought Dorothy really showed some riding talent. I thought, 'Oh, horrors! I've got a talented child!' " The adults burst out laughing.

"I don't understand," Carole said, frowning. "Why would that be horrible?" Stevie and Lisa grinned. They were both good riders, but they knew that Carole wanted someday to be far better than good.

"Oh, the work!" explained Mrs. DeSoto. "Think about it—I had to put up with Dorothy going down to that stable every day. I had to endure muddy boots on my carpet and muddy breeches in the wash. I knew that soon I'd be spending my Saturdays at horse shows, and eventually I'd probably have to buy her a horse!"

She laughed again, and this time Carole laughed with her. She hadn't ever thought about her riding from her father's point of view. "I bet you were just as understanding of Dorothy's riding as my dad is of mine," she said.

"Well, yes," admitted Mrs. DeSoto. "But those first few minutes were terrifying."

Stevie turned away from the table and looked out the window again. Raindrops made tracks down the glass, and the sky was dark gray. She wondered if it was raining at Pine Hollow. Ever since she'd gotten up that morning, she'd worried about Belle. Red had promised to turn Belle out when they were gone, and first Stevie had worried that he hadn't done it, that Belle was pining and restless in her stall. Now she worried that Red had left Belle out in the cold rain, and Belle was wet and unhappy.

Stevie sighed and leaned her head against the window. Belle had been miserable the last day they spent together—the last ride they had had, when Stevie had tried to force her to do a flying change. No, Stevie corrected herself, I tried to *teach* her a flying change.

No, she corrected herself again, more honestly, I tried to *force* her to do a flying change. She sighed again. She loved her horse so much. She didn't know what to do! No matter how much fun she had on Chincoteague, Stevie couldn't stop thinking about Belle. If only Belle would do a flying change!

Lisa saw the anguished look on her friend's face. She touched Carole's arm and pointed to Stevie, and Carole nodded sadly. No matter how much they tried to get Stevie's mind off Belle, clearly it wasn't working. Stevie was miserable.

The next afternoon, Nigel and Mrs. DeSoto went to
the mainland to shop at a wholesale club for kitchen
and bathroom supplies for the inn. Dorothy planned
to go shopping for bed and bath linens to match the
inn's guest rooms. Denise volunteered to go with her.
Only The Saddle Club and Mrs. Reg were left on
Chincoteague.

"Well," said Mrs. Reg, laying down her copy of the
island's weekly newspaper, "it gives the name of a
store here that rents bicycles. Wouldn't that be a nice
way for us to get to Assateague?"

The Saddle Club quickly agreed. Half an hour later,

mounted on bicycles, the four rode across the bridge to the outer island.

"What I'd like to do is explore the lighthouse," Mrs. Reg declared. "After that, you girls can take over and show me your favorite spots." They left their bicycles on the edge of the parking lot across from the Visitors' Center and began the short walk uphill to the red-and-white-striped lighthouse.

"Stevie, are you limping?" Mrs. Reg asked, her voice tinged with concern.

Stevie shrugged. She'd been trying not to show it, but her leg was still a little sore. "A wild pony kicked me," she confessed, "but it was my fault." She pulled the leg of her shorts up and showed Mrs. Reg the yellowing bruise. "It's not serious; it's just sore."

Mrs. Reg examined the bruise and nodded. "Around horses, it's easy for things to be the rider's fault," she said. "Do be careful, Stevie." She gave Stevie a sympathetic look and continued walking.

As usual, Stevie wasn't sure what Mrs. Reg meant, but she was glad Mrs. Reg wasn't angry at her. She was a bit glad, too, that Mrs. Reg had found out about the accident.

"Mrs. Reg, do you believe in the Spanish galleon?" Carole asked.

"I certainly believe in Spanish galleons in general,"

Mrs. Reg said. "Did you have a particular one in mind?"

Carole grinned. "The one that was supposed to have wrecked off Assateague and left the ponies here," she said. "Do you think it's true?"

"I don't," Lisa cut in. "I enjoy reading about it that way, but I think the other story Denise told us—the one about the colonial horses escaping and banding together—makes more sense. It fits the available facts better."

"But what if the facts aren't available?" Stevie asked her. "The way I see it, the fact is if a ship sank, there aren't any facts. Or if there are, they're down on the bottom of the ocean with the rest of the ship."

"But I really think it could be true," Carole persisted. "If the ship is on the bottom of the ocean, that's a fact, isn't it?"

"*If* it is," Lisa said. "And I think if it were down there, someone would have found it by now. And since no one has, it isn't there. And therefore—"

"But think about it, Lisa," countered Carole. "A whole shipful of ponies, worth their weight in gold, headed to a horrible life in the South American gold mines, and instead they get caught in a terrible storm, a hurricane, maybe—"

"Oh, definitely, make it a hurricane," said Stevie.

Carole ignored her and went on, "—and then they

land on this wonderful island, with fresh water, sandy beaches, and good marsh grass, everything they need to live—"

"—happily ever after," Lisa concluded. "It's romantic, like a fairy tale, and that makes it a good story. But I don't think that the best story is always the truth." They had reached the lighthouse but discovered that it was locked. "I thought they'd have a lighthouse keeper," Lisa said, sounding disappointed. "Isn't that the way it works in books?"

"Now who's reading too many books!" Stevie said, laughing. "Lisa, it's electric. Automatic. They probably had a lighthouse keeper here a hundred years ago."

"A lighthouse was first built on this location in the 1830s," Mrs. Reg said, reading the sign near the door. "And they have a local art exhibit up here on weekends. Too bad we won't be staying past Friday." They walked around the base of the lighthouse, exploring.

"But back to what you said before, Lisa," said Stevie. "About the most interesting story not always being the truth. Just because a story's interesting doesn't mean it can't be true. You shouldn't believe that the ponies came from the colonists just because that's the most boring explanation we have."

"I still think the ponies came from a wrecked Spanish galleon," Carole said stubbornly.

"I don't think it matters at all where the ponies

came from," Mrs. Reg interjected suddenly. "All horses are basically the same."

The Saddle Club stared at her in disbelief. "You can't mean that!" Stevie said.

"Starlight," Carole cut in indignantly, "is nothing at all like Patch!" Patch was one of the oldest and gentlest—and least athletic and least exciting—horses at Pine Hollow.

"And all the different breeds of horses are different from one another," Lisa said. "Thoroughbreds are fast and athletic; quarter horses are agile and strong—"

Mrs. Reg held up her hand. "All right, all right! I didn't mean it quite that way! What I meant was, all horses are horses. They all act like horses, and they all think like horses." She paused, frowning as she looked for the right words to explain what she meant. "They all have the same instincts," she finally said, "and they all have the same basic needs."

The Saddle Club couldn't find a way to argue with that, although none of them was exactly sure what Mrs. Reg meant.

"You mean," Carole said at last, "a horse will never act like a cow?"

"Right," said Mrs. Reg. "That's exactly it. A horse is a horse is a horse."

"Horses and cows are a little bit alike," Carole said thoughtfully.

"Sure, they both eat grass," Stevie said. "I eat apples, and so does Belle, but that doesn't make me a horse! I guess I understand what you mean, Mrs. Reg, but I'm not sure that it matters. The wild ponies still had to come from somewhere. One of the stories must be true."

They began heading back down the trail. An opening in the brush gave them a clear view of the beach fronting the Assateague Channel below. Another band of wild ponies played on the sand, and the girls and Mrs. Reg stopped to watch them.

"Look at the foals!" Carole cried. One pinto baby darted out of the pack of horses and began to gallop across the sand. Looking over his shoulder, he suddenly seemed to realize how far he was away from his mother. He wheeled around so quickly that he almost stumbled, and went galloping back to her side. Another pair of foals reared up, nuzzling each other in mock battle, and a piebald mare gave a great heaving sigh and flung herself down on the sand to roll with abandon. She stood up, shaking herself, and sand flew in all directions. The foals shied away.

Without warning the band took off, galloping madly across the sand. The mares leaped incoming waves, and the stallion, at the rear, trumpeted. They ran until they were nearly out of sight—the girls could see glints of sunlight from far down the beach as the horses splashed in the surf.

"Why do you think they did that?" Stevie asked, a note of awe in her voice. "I didn't see anything to scare them."

Lisa and Carole shook their heads. Mrs. Reg laughed. "Why would they need a reason?" she asked. "It looked like they were having fun."

"Fun?" Stevie asked. Her eyes took on a faraway, unhappy look. Carole nudged Lisa, who nodded.

Everything they did reminded Stevie of Belle.

THE NEXT DAY was their last on the islands. The Saddle Club helped Dorothy and Nigel hang curtains in all of the newly painted guest rooms. Then they helped Mrs. Reg plant geraniums along the brick path to the front door. At lunchtime, Mrs. DeSoto handed them three large paper bags. "You girls have been such a big help this week," she said. "I don't know what we would have done without you. So I made you a little picnic lunch—it's a specialty of the DeSoto Inn!"

The Saddle Club agreed that they'd like nothing more than to take their picnic to the beach on Assateague. They told Mrs. Reg where they were going, rented bicycles in town, and headed for the ocean. The beach was less crowded than it had been the first time they visited it, and they quickly found a secluded spot on the sand to enjoy Mrs. DeSoto's delicacies.

"I'm starving!" Carole said, spreading the contents of her bag—a fancy sandwich with the crusts removed, a salad in a little plastic box, a fresh peach, soda, and a handful of shortbread cookies—out onto her beach towel. "Boy, does this look good! Don't you think so?"

"It sure does!" Lisa opened her soda and took a big swallow. "Stevie?" She noticed that her friend hadn't opened her lunch. "Aren't you hungry?"

Stevie looked up. "Oh, sure," she said. Lisa and Carole frowned. Stevie had been strangely quiet ever since the wild mare had kicked her. She'd stared out the window for most of the afternoon that they'd spent making cookies. Even yesterday with Mrs. Reg, she hadn't acted like her usual rambunctious self. Now she wasn't interested in lunch! It wasn't like her at all.

"Are you feeling okay?" Carole asked. "Are you sure that pony didn't hurt you worse than you're telling us? Or is it Belle?"

"You should tell us," Lisa said gently. "Stevie, whatever's bothering you, we want to help."

For a moment Stevie looked surprised; then she smiled at her friends. "I'm not hurt," she said. "I've been trying to act like nothing's been wrong, but I guess you two know me too well for that to work. But I'm not hurt—if anything, that pony kick helped bring me to my senses." She pushed her lunch bag aside and her smile dissolved. "Lisa, Carole, I've been so worried! What if I've really messed up? I wanted to catch up with Phil so much that I forgot how important my horse is! What if somehow I've really *hurt* Belle?"

Lisa thought that Stevie looked ready to cry. She leaned over and put her arms around her friend.

"You didn't hurt her," Lisa said. "Belle knows how much you love her. I'm sure she's okay."

"I'm sure, too," Carole said, reaching over and giving Stevie's arm a squeeze.

Stevie wiped a few stray tears from her eyes. "Really? Do you really think so?" She looked up at Carole. Carole knew so much about horses—why hadn't she asked Carole for help before?

"I really do," Carole said. "In the first place, you were exasperated with Belle, but you were never abusive to her. There's a big difference between not training a horse entirely correctly and training it incorrectly. And second, you weren't asking her to do anything that's beyond what she can do. At this stage in her training, Belle should be more than ready to do a flying change. In fact, I'm kind of surprised she hasn't already been taught to do it."

"Plus," Lisa added, "you've only been pushing Belle

hard for one week. You may have gotten her a little bit upset, but it hasn't been going on for very long, and she had this whole week off to relax. She'll be happy and rested when we get back, and tomorrow the two of you can start over."

Stevie smiled tremulously. "I've been so worried over the past few days," she confessed. "I was really afraid that I had hurt her. I was afraid I'd go home and she'd hate me and not want to do anything that I asked her to at all. And then I was afraid that I wasn't a good rider, and didn't deserve my own horse, and then I was afraid that Belle wasn't as good a horse as I thought she was—" She sighed. "Just telling you all this has made me feel a little bit better already."

"Belle's a terrific horse," Lisa said. "And you're a good rider. This was just one mistake."

"Thanks." Stevie returned Lisa's hug. "Did you really mean what you said, Carole? You really don't think I've hurt her?"

"Of course," Carole said. "You didn't hurt her."

"Good. I should have asked you for help a long time ago."

"I should have helped without your asking," Carole replied. "I did try, sort of, but—" But I got angry instead, Carole thought, feeling a little ashamed of herself. The Saddle Club was supposed to stick together.

They lay back in the sunshine. "I feel better enough

109

to tackle a sandwich now," Stevie said, opening her lunch. "So, okay, tomorrow I'll go home and ride Belle again, only with a different attitude. I don't want to lose my temper with her, but I do want her to eventually learn a flying change. I know that I was pushing her too hard, and I know that my reason for wanting her to do it—because I wanted to be just as good as Phil—wasn't a good one, but, no matter what, I *still* don't understand why she hasn't learned a change. We did those exercises for *hours*." She bit down on her sandwich emphatically.

"Hmmm," Carole said, crossing her hands behind her head and thinking hard. She knew Belle ought to be able to do a flying change. "Well, Stevie," she said at last, "maybe you aren't looking at the exercises from Belle's point of view. You got them out of training books, didn't you?"

"Yes, but they're very good books," Stevie said. "Max told me I should read them sometime anyway, and—"

Carole held up her hand to stop her. "No, I know they're good books, and they're probably very good exercises. That's not what I mean."

Both Stevie and Lisa looked confused. "What *do* you mean?" Lisa asked.

"Let me think—it's not really easy to explain." Lisa and Stevie grinned. Carole could sound very confused

110

when she wasn't talking about horses—it was a new experience for her to be confused when she *was* talking about horses.

"Okay," Carole said, after a short pause, "it's this. You read the book, so you know that the exercises are supposed to make Belle do a flying change, right?"

"Right," Stevie said. "In the one I like best, the second one I tried, you pick up a canter, canter through a corner, then turn and double back through the same corner but going in the wrong direction. The horse is supposed to get thrown off balance by the turn on the wrong lead and do a flying change in order to get its balance back." A seagull landed next to Stevie, and she tossed it a bit of cookie. Startled, it flew away.

"That's just what I thought," Carole said. "It's exactly what I mean. *You* know the exercise is supposed to make her do a flying change, but *Belle* doesn't know it."

Stevie thought for a moment and then grinned, her face lighting up. "I get it!" she said. "I read in the book, 'this is how to teach your horse to do flying changes,' but Belle didn't! She thinks I'm just asking her to change directions at the canter, and, as far as she can tell, she's doing exactly what I want!"

"I get it, too," said Lisa, her face shining. "I didn't at first, but you're right, Carole. You know how Prancer gets upset whenever I yell at her for doing

111

something wrong? Belle's sensitive in exactly the same way. Belle knows you're upset with her, but she thinks she's doing what you want, so she gets upset right back at you. In her mind you aren't being fair." She leaned back and dug her toes into the sand. "Wow. That was complicated, sort of, but I think we all understand it now." For a few moments they all ate their lunches. Lisa began to pack their trash into one of the paper bags.

"I think that understanding Belle was the whole key," Stevie said a few minutes later, "but my next question is, what can I do to help her do a change? I've been shifting my weight in the saddle to try to make her feel even more unbalanced. Do you think that's a good idea?"

"No, probably not," Carole replied. She wiped the peach juice off her chin and threw the pit into Lisa's trash bag. "See, you want to make this as stress-free for Belle as possible. You want to keep doing the exercises but without getting angry at her. Eventually she'll do a change by accident, because it really will be more comfortable for her to go through the corner on the other canter lead. Once she does it, you'll praise her and keep on doing it. Then she'll come to understand that the flying change is the point of the exercise, and then you can teach her to do it off of a leg cue, like Teddy does."

"Whew," said Stevie. "Sounds like a lot of work."

"No more work than you've already been doing," Lisa replied. "I never saw you work so hard on any one thing before."

"I guess that's true. And anyway, it sounds like it's something I can do—it sounds a whole lot better than the way I was trying to do it last week."

"You needed to see it from Belle's point of view," Lisa repeated thoughtfully. "That's good advice, Carole. That sounds like something Denise would say."

Stevie drained her can of soda and stood up. "If you've finished eating," she said, "I'd really like to go back to the woodland trail. Since the pony kicked me partway through, we never got to explore the rest of it."

"Sounds great." They packed up their trash and threw it away in the big container by the parking lot where they'd left their bikes. They rode away from the ocean, past another tidewater pool teeming with birds.

"I wouldn't mind seeing that blue heron again," Stevie commented. "He looked like he'd know something about everything—he looked like an old professor or one of the ancient Latin teachers at Fenton Hall. You guys are lucky not to have to take Latin where you go to school."

"I'd take Latin if it were taught by a heron," Carole said with a grin.

They locked their bikes around a small pine tree just outside the entrance to the trail.

"I'm glad there aren't too many people here," Lisa said, as they began to walk through the shady trees.

"Me too," Carole agreed. "You know, I really wanted everything about Chincoteague and Assateague to be just the same as in the *Misty* books. I didn't expect the bridges or the cars, or all the tourists on the beach. I guess I'd forgotten how long ago the books were written. But when we get out by ourselves here on Assateague, I can forget all the modern stuff. I can imagine it any way that I want." She smiled mischievously. "And when I look out at the ocean, I can see that Spanish galleon."

Lisa laughed. "Usually I'm the one with too much imagination!"

"Last night Denise told me a little bit more about this natural horsemanship," Stevie said. She walked first down the trail and held a thorny branch out of the way for her friends.

"Denise thinks that if you're training your horse for a specific event—say, show jumping—you should only spend twenty percent of your riding time actually jumping fences," Stevie continued. "The other eighty percent should be spent doing more general riding, or having fun with your horse, so that your horse stays relaxed and happy." She grinned. "I guess if I apply

114

this rule to teaching Belle a flying change, it means I'll be spending a lot less time on those exercises—and a lot more time on the trail!"

"Yeah!" cheered Lisa. "It didn't feel right when we went without you."

"It didn't feel right to me, either," Stevie admitted.

"We'll help you with Belle," Carole promised. "I don't think it's important that she learn to do a flying change before next week, but I'd really like to help you teach it to her."

Stevie swung her arms and tossed her ponytail over her shoulder happily. "I wish I'd listened to the two of you earlier," she said. "I would have enjoyed this week more. Doesn't the air smell crisp? I love pine trees."

"You might have been more willing to listen if Lisa and I had been more willing to talk," Carole admitted. "I shouldn't have yelled at you that one day. The Saddle Club has to stick together."

"I think we do pretty well," Stevie said. She felt so happy she was ready to sing. But, knowing how her singing voice sounded, she thought she would spare her friends. Not to mention the animals! After all, this was supposed to be a wildlife *refuge*. She wondered if she could get kicked off Assateague for scaring them. The thought made her giggle.

They rounded the bend to the clearing where they had seen the wild ponies before. "I wonder if we'll see—" Lisa began. "Oh," she said, dropping her voice to a whisper. "There they are!"

"Careful, Stevie," Carole warned, but Stevie didn't need warning. A small band stood on the far edge of the clearing, in a patch of sandy marshland. Stevie knew she had never seen these particular wild ponies before, but she also knew, as soon as she saw them, exactly what she was going to do.

I've learned a lot on Chincoteague, she thought. These wild ponies have taught me as much as any well-trained horse ever did. Quietly, slowly, she walked across the clearing toward the band. Carole started to follow, but Lisa held her back.

Stevie picked out a young brown-and-white pinto mare grazing at the edge of the band. The mare had a scruffy mane and rough, unkempt coat, but her expression was alert and kind. She watched Stevie cautiously, but she didn't seem afraid.

"Steady, girl," Stevie said soothingly. She stood still for a moment, giving the mare and the rest of the band a chance to get used to her. Then she walked a few more steps forward and held out her hand. The mare raised her head and sniffed it. "Good girl," Stevie said. Gently she began to rub the mare's neck. The mare leaned into Stevie's hand and half closed her eyes. Stevie rubbed a little harder, her fingers raising dust from the mare's coat. The mare dropped her head and bit off another mouthful of grass, then raised her head and looked Stevie in the eye. Stevie patted the mare's forehead.

The mare blinked, then took a small step backward. Stevie held her hand out to her. The mare began to edge away, back toward the other members of her band. Stevie dropped her hand and let her go. "Good girl," she said again. The mare stopped and looked at her curiously. "See?" Stevie said to her. "I'm not really so scary—and you're not that wild after all."

12

STEVIE LEANED OUT the window of the horse van and waved. "Happy Birthday, Phil!" she cried. Red eased the van to a halt in the Marstens' driveway next to their barn, and Stevie hopped out. She hurried to let Belle out of the rear. "Thanks so much, Red," she said. "I really appreciate this."

Red grinned. "I'll be back to pick you up at four o'clock," he said. "And you can muck out those twenty stalls for me anytime you want."

Phil helped her lift the unloading ramp back into place. "I wondered how you would manage to bring Belle here," he said. "Am I really worth mucking out twenty stalls?"

"Only on your birthday," Stevie told him. "Besides, Belle and I have got a problem that we need your help with."

"Belle's allergies haven't come back, have they?" Phil asked, his voice concerned.

"No—and if you'll remember, I helped you with that one, not the other way around! No, this is something different—wait, Red!" The van was starting to pull away. Red stopped when he heard Stevie's shriek. He opened his door and asked her what was wrong.

"The picnic!" Stevie said, running to open the passenger door. "I almost forgot our lunch!"

"You wouldn't want to do that, not with what you brought," Red agreed, laughing. "Or at least, I wouldn't want you leaving it in my truck!" Stevie grabbed her backpack and shut the door, and Red drove away.

"What did you bring?" Phil asked.

"It's a specialty—a Stevie Lake Specialty!"

Phil groaned. "I hope it isn't like your ice cream sundaes," he said. "Even I don't see how you can stand to eat those!"

"It's a very nice lunch," Stevie said defensively. "And if you don't like it, you can feed it to Teddy!"

"Oh, no—you brought me oats and apples!"

Stevie stuck out her tongue. "I'm not even going to show you," she said.

"You didn't dye everything green, did you? Because I seem to remember you serving me green hamburgers once. Or purple—Stevie, promise me it's not all purple!"

Stevie laughed. "The green hamburgers were my brother's fault," she said. "If I remember correctly, you ate them. A little food coloring never hurt anyone." She swung her backpack onto her shoulder and took Belle's lead rope away from Phil. "Let's go get Teddy. I'm dying to get in the saddle."

"You didn't dye your saddle purple, did you?"

Stevie rolled her eyes. "I'm going to ignore everything you say," she said.

Phil turned and slipped his hand around her waist. "Will you ignore this, Stevie?" he asked, his face close to hers. "I'm very glad that you came to spend my birthday with me, I'm very glad you think seeing me is worth mucking out twenty stalls, and I'm going to show you just how glad I am." He leaned forward to kiss her. Stevie closed her eyes.

"Phil! Phil-lip!" Phil sprang away from Stevie. Stevie's eyes flew open. Phil's mother came around the corner of the barn with a tattered knapsack in her hands. "Oh, there you are. Hello, Stevie, it's always nice to see you. Phil, I packed the two of you a little lunch, just in case"—she glanced doubtfully at Stevie —"just in case you're still hungry after—anyway, dear, have a nice time." She handed the knapsack to Phil and walked back to the house.

"I understand why you don't entirely trust my lunch," Stevie said thoughtfully. "After all, you did have to eat a green hamburger. But I don't understand why your mother doesn't trust my lunch."

Phil shrugged. "Maybe she heard about the green hamburgers."

They took Belle into the barn. Stevie had groomed her and tacked her up before putting her in the trailer, and Phil had already groomed Teddy. Within minutes they were in the saddle. Phil signaled Teddy to walk.

"Before we go out to the trails, Phil," Stevie said, "remember—"

"That's right." Phil pulled Teddy up. "You wanted to ask me about something, didn't you? Something to do with Belle?"

"I thought maybe we could use your outdoor ring," Stevie said, riding Belle toward the small, sand-filled arena next to the Marstens' barn. "You see, Phil, I'm having trouble teaching Belle to do a flying lead change." Stevie sighed. "I've been going through some exercises with her, but we're still having trouble. You've done such a great job with Teddy. Can you help?"

Phil blinked. Slowly a big smile spread across his face. "Gosh, Stevie, I'd be glad to," he said. "It's kind of a new experience, your asking me for help. I'm glad that you thought to ask me. What exactly have you and Belle been doing?"

Stevie briefly described the exercise she'd discussed with Carole and Lisa. Phil nodded. "That sounds like it should work," he said. "Let's see you ride it."

Stevie walked Belle a few times around the arena, then trotted her several laps in both directions to be sure her muscles were warm and loose. Then she asked Belle to canter and went through the exercise, changing directions in a tight, s-shaped curve. Belle didn't change leads, but, Stevie noticed, she was a lot more relaxed than she had been last week.

It's because I'm not getting angry at her for something she can't understand, Stevie thought. She could feel, too, a difference in her own riding—now that she wasn't getting angry with Belle, her legs, seat, and hands all felt softer, and her balance was better, too. Much more like dressage, Stevie thought. She knew that in the very high-level dressage exhibitions she had seen, the rider's cues to the horse were practically invisible. Today she was being much less obvious with her own cues, and Belle was certainly more relaxed. But Belle still wasn't doing a flying lead change.

"See." Stevie pulled Belle up to the rail near Phil and Teddy. "Last week I was upsetting her, although I didn't mean to. Now at least she's pretty calm about it.

But she's still not getting it. I tried to sort of shift my weight and throw her off balance, but all that did was harass her."

Phil agreed. "You don't want to upset her," he said. "But the way you're riding now, she can still manage to canter on the wrong lead all the way through the turn. Maybe you should make your circles smaller. Ask her to turn really tightly, and maybe that will make enough of a difference." He grinned. "She canters really well, Stevie. She's a beautiful mover. Not like Teddy—he's a great horse cross-country, and he does everything I ask, but he's nowhere near as elegant. Belle's going to be really good at dressage someday."

Stevie glowed at his praise. This was a new thing— she was asking Phil for help, and not only was he helping, but he was being awfully nice about it. Stevie vowed to let this be a lesson to her. Next time she wouldn't get so caught up in competing with Phil. She'd remember what a really good friend he could be.

"I like your idea," she said. "Should we try it?"

Phil nodded. "Go ahead. I'm in no hurry to eat lunch anyway. It's probably hot pink potato chips, navy blue lunch meat—"

Stevie made a face and trotted Belle away. She asked for a canter just before the corner. Belle lifted easily into the faster gait and bent smoothly through the turn. Immediately Stevie asked her to continue

123

turning and double back the way she had come. Belle tried hard to keep her smooth bend, but when the circle changed direction she nearly stumbled. Stevie sat as quietly as she could. Belle took another off-balance stride, then, suddenly, made a sort of skipping leap, and, smooth again, continued through the rest of the turn.

Stevie glanced down. Belle was on the other lead! She looked up at Phil, her eyes wide with joy. "Was that it?" she asked. "That sort of hop?"

Phil laughed. "That was it, Stevie Lake. Your first flying change."

"Wow." Stevie halted and bent forward in the saddle to throw her arms around Belle. "You wonderful, wonderful mare," she said, patting Belle's neck and ruffling her mane. "That was it! That was very good!"

"Try it again," Phil suggested. "Give her a chance to learn that that's what she's supposed to do."

"That was it, Belle," Stevie told her. "Once more, and we'll hit the trails." Again she trotted toward the corner and picked up a canter. She rode the turn back exactly as she had before.

This time, Belle was different. This time, Stevie realized, Belle understood. She didn't stumble or fuss. At exactly the point where the circle changed directions, Belle did a flying change.

Stevie pulled her up and dismounted. She threw her

arms around Belle. "I knew you could do it," she said. "I knew you could."

"Well, of course she could," Phil cut in. "A fine athletic horse like Belle and a terrific rider like you— of course she could."

Stevie grinned up at him and Teddy. "It took a little more than that," she said. "It took some wild ponies, and some help from some very good friends."

"You'll have to explain about the wild ponies," Phil told her. "But you've always got friends, Stevie. You never need to face any of your problems alone."

Stevie led Belle out of the Marstens' ring and latched the gate. She shrugged herself into her backpack and remounted. "Let's go have that picnic!" she said. "Now we've got two things to celebrate— your birthday and Belle's flying change!"

13

"So what color did you make the lunch?" Lisa asked.
"Violent violet? Fuchsia? Chartreuse?" She slid into
The Saddle Club's favorite booth at TD's. The three
of them had agreed to meet at Pine Hollow and walk
to TD's right after Stevie got back from Phil's birthday
ride. Lisa and Carole were eager to hear the details.

"I didn't color anything," Stevie protested indignantly. "All of you, even Phil, seem to think that I'm
incapable of making an elegant picnic lunch. In fact,
all I did was copy the lunch Mrs. DeSoto gave us on
our last day at Assateague—to a T!"

"Then why would Red say what he said?" Carole

asked. On the walk from Pine Hollow to TD's, Stevie had already told them about most of her day.

Stevie grinned. "That was Red's idea of a joke. Well, actually, I sort of put him up to it. I thought it would be funny if Phil was just a little worried. That way, he'd really appreciate it when my lunch turned out so nice!"

"And did it?" Lisa asked.

Stevie grimaced. "The colors were all right," she said. "And I didn't mess up the sodas or peaches— except the sodas got shaken up during the ride, so when Phil opened his it kind of squirted him in the face."

"Kind of?" Carole raised her eyebrows.

"Yeah." Stevie nodded. "Teddy backed up so fast, I was afraid he was going to break a rein. Phil was holding him. On the ground, fortunately. Belle didn't spook at all."

"She's used to you," Lisa said. "So, the peaches were all right?"

Stevie sighed and took a minute to study the menu intently. Carole and Lisa exchanged glances over the top of her head. Stevie knew the menu at TD's better than anyone in Pine Hollow!

"What happened to the peaches?" Carole asked.

"*I* didn't mess them up," Stevie said. "But they got a little bruised—I guess they got bumped around with the sodas. The horses liked them." She bit her lip and began to giggle. "It was the rest of it," she said, giving in to great whoops of laughter. "I wanted to be elegant —and I got the colors right—it was the *flavors* I got all wrong!"

Stevie pounded the table and laughed. Carole and Lisa felt mystified. Their usual waitress approached them, with a determined frown on her face. "What's she laughing about now?" she asked, jabbing her pen toward Stevie.

"We wish we knew," Carole told her. "She hasn't gotten around to telling us yet. But I'd like a hot fudge sundae."

Lisa ordered a vanilla shake. Stevie sat up. "In honor of my gourmet cooking," she said, "I'll take a scoop of peach ice cream with pineapple sauce and black licorice sprinkles." The waitress nodded grimly —she was used to Stevie's strange combinations—and walked away. Lisa and Carole looked dumbfounded.

"Now you've got to tell us," Lisa told Stevie sternly.

"I'm just lucky they don't have horseradish-flavored ice cream," Stevie said. "Otherwise I'd have to order that, too. Can you believe what I did? First I used horseradish sauce instead of mayonnaise on the sandwiches. Really strong horseradish sauce that my grandmother makes, that makes tears come to your eyes when you eat the littlest bit of it—and I used a lot, because I know Phil likes mayonnaise!"

"Poor Phil," Carole said sympathetically.

"Yeah. He took a really big bite. But in a way that was sort of good, because then he couldn't taste the cookies. I made sugar cookies. I must have grabbed the wrong bottle. I think I used anise instead of vanilla."

"Anise?" Carole frowned.

"Licorice flavoring," Lisa supplied.

"Right." Stevie nodded her head. "They looked great—little rocking horse cookies—but they tasted *awful*. And then I made a salad, just like Mrs. DeSoto did, and Phil made me taste that first so he didn't get any. I'm going to have to ask my mom what that stuff in the refrigerator was. I thought it was salad dressing. It tasted like pineapple juice."

"Good thing we came to TD's. You must be hungry."

"Oh, Phil's mother packed us a lunch, too," Stevie said cheerfully. "And her sodas exploded, too, so I didn't feel so bad. And I don't think Phil really cared. I know I didn't. After Belle did that flying change, everything was wonderful. The day was just perfect."

Stevie described again the exact way that Belle had felt when she did her flying change. Lisa and Carole had already heard the same description three times, once in the barn at Pine Hollow, while Stevie put

129

Belle away, and twice on the walk to TD's, but they listened happily. They both knew how incredibly good Stevie felt.

"Best of all, I think she'll be able to do them from now on," Stevie concluded. "I'll work on it with her a little bit every time I ride, so she learns how to do them whenever I ask, but I really think she understands. I think our problems are over—at least as far as the flying change is concerned."

The waitress brought their ice cream, and Stevie dug in happily. "I don't know how you can eat that," Carole remarked.

"It's good," Stevie said. "Want some?" Carole shuddered and took a big bite of hot fudge.

"I think what Denise told me about natural horsemanship helped a lot," Stevie continued, "because it kind of taught me a different way of thinking about horse training. It taught me to be a little more patient and to pay more attention to Belle's reactions."

"I liked it, too," Carole said. "No matter how much I learn about horses, it seems like I've always got a whole lot more to learn. Maybe we can get Denise to teach us more about natural horsemanship."

"I bet she'd be happy to help us," Lisa said. "We can ask her tomorrow."

"There's only one thing still bothering me about last week," Stevie said, scraping her spoon across the bottom of her dish to catch every drop of syrup and licorice, "and that's what Mrs. Reg did about the horse in her story—Madeleine, the one that wouldn't jump? I thought about that horse the whole time we were on Chincoteague. It made me think that, whatever mistakes I was making with Belle, they weren't irreversible—but I'd like to know what really did happen."

"I bet Mrs. Reg just backed off to wherever the horse was comfortable and started training again from there," Carole guessed. "That's what I would do. Maybe jumped her over ground poles and little-bitty fences for a while—"

"That's what she did do," Lisa cut in. She grinned at the looks of surprise on her friends' faces. "I mean, that's what I thought she probably did, and I knew she would never tell us on her own, so today I asked her."

"Did she tell you about it?" Carole asked.

Lisa shook her head. "You know Mrs. Reg. She said, 'Of course, Lisa—and isn't Prancer's water getting a little bit low? You might refill it for her.'" The Saddle Club laughed. That sounded like Mrs. Reg.

"And Mrs. Reg got a phone call from Mrs. DeSoto," Lisa continued. "Thanks to all our help, the DeSoto Inn is almost ready for guests. The furniture is coming tomorrow, and they expect to be fully operational in a week. They're already booked solid for the Pony Penning!"

"That's one good thing that came out of our trip," Carole said, "and what Stevie learned about Belle is another. But have either of you noticed the third good thing?"

Stevie looked puzzled. Lisa nodded. "Max," she said.

"Max," Carole confirmed. "While you were on your picnic, Stevie, and Lisa and I were taking care of Starlight, Veronica came in ten minutes late for a lesson."

"Max didn't yell?"

"He hardly even cared. He was so understanding about it that I think Veronica was a little embarrassed. And he walks around whistling."

"He told me that he canceled some of his lessons while we were gone," Lisa said. "Deborah said that they took some long picnic rides themselves and slept late in the mornings. I guess all Max needed was a little bit more honeymoon!" She drank the last of her shake.

"So, Stevie," Carole said, leaning back in the booth. "You got your wish. You and Belle gave Phil a flying change for his birthday."

Stevie blushed. "Do you know what Phil said?" she asked. "He said his real birthday present was that I let him help me with Belle. But what I actually gave him —besides my delicious picnic—was a book on dressage, that Bert de Némethy book on horse training. And I figure, now that Belle and I can do flying changes, we've got Phil and Teddy beat. He's going to need all the help he can get!" She winked at her friends, who laughed appreciatively. Stevie was doing pretty well when she could joke about her own competitiveness.

"Let me get this straight," Lisa said. "You bought a book for Phil's birthday, and then you read it to find help for Belle. Sounds like it was a present for you, too!"

Stevie waved her hand. "That's completely unimportant," she said. "But, oh, I can't tell you how wonderful it feels when she does a flying change. It's not much—it's just a lift, like a little jump, but not really —it's the best feeling in the world!" Stevie raised her water glass. "I want to make a toast," she declared. "To The Saddle Club, my good friends, for helping me, and especially to my beautiful flying horse!"

ABOUT THE AUTHOR

BONNIE BRYANT is the author of many books for young readers, including novelizations of movie hits such as *Teenage Mutant Ninja Turtles* and *Honey, I Blew Up the Kid*, written under her married name, B. B. Hiller.

Ms. Bryant began writing The Saddle Club in 1986. Although she had done some riding before that, she intensified her studies then, and found herself learning right along with her characters Stevie, Carole, and Lisa. She claims that they are all much better riders than she is.

Ms. Bryant was born and raised in New York City and still lives there, in Greenwich Village, with her two sons.

THE SADDLE CLUB ™

❑ 15594-6 HORSE CRAZY #1	$3.50/$4.50 Can.	❑ 15938-0 STAR RIDER #19	$3.50/$4.50 Can.
❑ 15611-X HORSE SHY #2	$3.25/$3.99 Can.	❑ 15907-0 SNOW RIDE #20	$3.50/$4.50 Can.
❑ 15626-8 HORSE SENSE #3	$3.50/$4.50 Can.	❑ 15983-6 RACEHORSE #21	$3.50/$4.50 Can.
❑ 15637-3 HORSE POWER #4	$3.50/$4.50 Can.	❑ 15990-9 FOX HUNT #22	$3.50/$4.50 Can.
❑ 15703-5 TRAIL MATES #5	$3.50/$4.50 Can.	❑ 48025-1 HORSE TROUBLE #23	$3.50/$4.50 Can.
❑ 15728-0 DUDE RANCH #6	$3.50/$4.50 Can.	❑ 48067-7 GHOST RIDER #24	$3.50/$4.50 Can.
❑ 15754-X HORSE PLAY #7	$3.25/$3.99 Can.	❑ 48072-3 SHOW HORSE #25	$3.50/$4.50 Can.
❑ 15769-8 HORSE SHOW #8	$3.25/$3.99 Can.	❑ 48073-1 BEACH RIDE #26	$3.50/$4.50 Can.
❑ 15780-9 HOOF BEAT #9	$3.50/$4.50 Can.	❑ 48074-X BRIDLE PATH #27	$3.50/$4.50 Can.
❑ 15790-6 RIDING CAMP #10	$3.50/$4.50 Can.	❑ 48075-8 STABLE MANNERS #28	$3.50/$4.50 Can.
❑ 15805-8 HORSE WISE #11	$3.25/$3.99 Can..	❑ 48076-6 RANCH HANDS #29	$3.50/$4.50 Can.
❑ 15821-X RODEO RIDER #12	$3.50/$4.50 Can.	❑ 48077-4 AUTUMN TRAIL #30	$3.50/$4.50 Can.
❑ 15832-5 STARLIGHT CHRISTMAS #13	$3.50/$4.50 Can.	❑ 48145-2 HAYRIDE #31	$3.50/$4.50 Can.
❑ 15847-3 SEA HORSE #14	$3.50/$4.50 Can.	❑ 48146-0 CHOCOLATE HORSE #32	$3.50/$4.50 Can.
❑ 15862-7 TEAM PLAY #15	$3.50/$4.50 Can.	❑ 48147-9 HIGH HORSE #33	$3.50/$4.50 Can.
❑ 15882-1 HORSE GAMES #16	$3.25/$3.99 Can.	❑ 48148-7 HAY FEVER #34	$3.50/$4.50 Can.
❑ 15937-2 HORSENAPPED #17	$3.50/$4.50 Can.	❑ 48149-5 A SUMMER WITHOUT	$3.99/$4.99 Can.
❑ 15928-3 PACK TRIP #18	$3.50/$4.50 Can.	HORSES Super #1